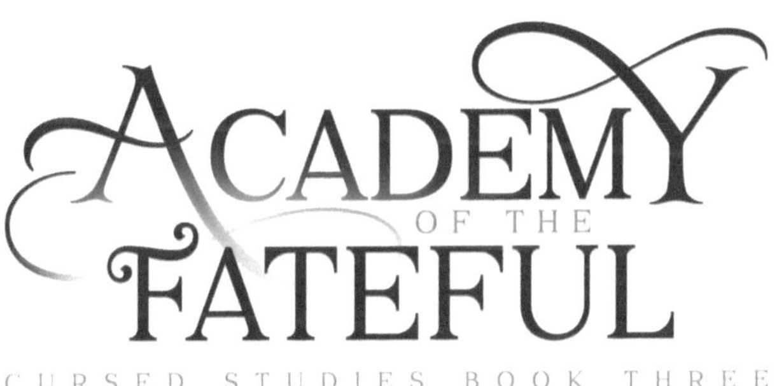

# ACADEMY OF THE FATEFUL

CURSED STUDIES BOOK THREE

## EVA CHASE

Academy of the Fateful

Book 3 in the Cursed Studies trilogy



This is a work of fiction. Any resemblance to actual persons, living or dead, or actual events is purely coincidental.

First Digital Edition, 2020



Cover design: Rebecca Frank, Bewitching Book Covers

Ebook ISBN: 978-1-989096-63-5

Paperback ISBN: 978-1-989096-64-2

 Created with Vellum

*Trix*

Roseborne College was an unsettling place at the best of times. Now, as I stood rigid outside the Victorian mansion's front door staring out at the havoc I'd unleashed, the campus might as well have been an outright horror show.

In the fading dusk, several students were tugging at the wrought-iron gate that led to the outside world, but it refused to release anything more than a creak of protest. A faintly glowing mist rolled off the rosebush that clung to the stone wall the rest of the way around campus. Ghostly figures formed from its haze, drifting toward the students by the gate and others scattered across the lawn.

A girl who'd been scrambling back to the school staggered as her legs wobbled beneath her. They gave out completely, pitching her onto the grass. Her breath was coming ragged. I peered across the lawn toward the wall, and a chill crept up my spine.

I couldn't make out much of the roses blooming there —the blooms that were somehow connected to the lives of each student—but in the mist's glow, one that I caught sight of shriveled tighter. Another let loose a couple of petals to drift toward the ground.

If a student's rose died, they died too. From what I'd gathered, that process usually took years while Roseborne's staff dealt out their tortures. It was speeding up before my eyes. Before, I'd thought there might be some small chance of using my gardening knowhow to strengthen the plant, but looking at it now, I had no hope at all that my skills could slow the flowers' decay.

I only had a few seconds to take in that problem before my gaze caught on a sight that made my heart lurch hard. One of the ghostly figures had come to a stop on the path between me and the gate. She turned toward me with a swing of her translucent but distinctive pitch-black hair. A filmy image of Sylvie, my foster brother's former girlfriend—the girl who'd *died* because of my jealousy— stared straight at me with kohl-lined eyes.

Holy shit. I backpedaled instinctively. My back smacked into the door that had closed behind me. Without thinking, driven by pure panic, I fumbled for the knob and pushed inside.

The situation in the foyer wasn't much more welcoming. A few students ran by me, pale-faced; another was huddled in a corner, hugging himself. Streaks of ghostly light glanced off the walls with a crackling energy that made the air thrum. In one, I caught a glimpse of the face of one of the eight students from nearly a century ago whose ritual had transformed this institution from an ordinary high school into a college driven by vengeance.

Their spirits had broken—or maybe been forced—out of the physical bodies they'd constructed to present themselves as the college's staff, but our tormenters obviously weren't gone. And who knew what the hell they had in store for us next.

They'd already unleashed some of that hell on the three guys who'd taken them on alongside me. If I could save anyone tonight, I had to save them. I dashed down the hall to the basement stairs.

In the laundry room, the person-sized hole I'd opened up in the far wall still gaped ominously. At the thought of the power that had welled up inside me and allowed me to crumble the concrete with my bare hands, my fingers curled into my palms. If I could have used the same trick on the outer wall, we'd all have had the chance to flee the campus right now.

But I couldn't. I felt the lack inside me with the same certainty as I'd known I could press through this wall less than an hour ago. The power that had come over me had faded away after the earlier mad rush of it. I couldn't have shattered a single brick, and I had no idea how to summon the energy again.

Roseborne's darkest secrets had waited beyond the opening in front of me—but so did Ryo, Jensen, and Elias, who'd helped me uncover those secrets and defended me while I tried to cut off the staff's source of power, and who might now be dying because of their allegiance to me. A jolt of urgency propelled me onward.

I stepped through the gap into the dim room. The light from the sconces along the walls flickered over the battered remains of the twisted rosebush I'd chopped to bits, revealing dark blood stains that marked the concrete floor beneath. Blood stains and the knife that'd opened up veins on eight pairs of wrists nearly a century ago, the blade now stabbed into the floor. I'd seen the macabre ritual the former students had conducted play out in a memory that wasn't entirely mine. I had some connection to one of those students-turned-spirits: Winston Baker, who might have been my great-grandfather.

Whatever power I'd temporarily wielded here, that had allowed me to enter this room and challenge his former allies' domination over Roseborne, I suspected he'd passed it on to me. But I hadn't been prepared for the chaos those actions would produce.

Voices—living human voices—carried from the hall beyond the scattered brambles. Dodging the splintered thorns, I hustled across the room.

Jenson and Ryo had managed to get Elias onto his feet. When I'd last seen him, our math teacher had been slumped on the floor. Elias appeared to be holding most of his own weight now, his well-muscled arms slung over the slimmer guys' shoulders only for balance, but the hard edges of his face stood out even more starkly with the hollowing of his cheeks and sudden sunkeness of his eyes.

He looked as though the life were draining out of him —the way my former roommate had looked in the last few days before her rose had crumbled away and her life had snuffed out at the same time.

"What's going on up there?" Jenson asked, his normally smooth voice taut with tension. He held his tall frame rigid beside Elias. From what I'd seen, there wasn't much love lost between the two of them—but he'd stayed to help the other guy anyway. With the way his bright blue eyes rested on me, I knew it hadn't really been for Elias's benefit. He'd come down here in the first place, faced the spirits' hostility and stood with the other guys I'd found myself falling for, because of how much he cared about me. That knowledge came with a bittersweet pang, knowing how far I was from seeing through the coup I'd been attempting.

"I'm not sure," I said. "Things have gotten… pretty wild. I don't think it's safe for any of us to stay down *here*, though. This was the center of the staff's power—they might still get something out of it."

"Getting out of here sounds good to me," Ryo said with a rough laugh. He ducked his head, the wavering light leaching the color from the vivid green streaks in his black hair. I thought I saw a shiver run through his lean body. Normally Ryo could find an optimistic spin on just about any situation—or at least a way to focus on something more upbeat as a distraction. His rose had been starting to show signs of age the last time I'd seen it, though. He'd been here almost three years. Was he starting to falter just like Elias was?

My stomach balled into a knot at the idea. I gave a brisk wave of my arm. "Come on. Let's see how things are upstairs and then decide where to go from there. The—the gate still won't open. We can't leave yet."

My plan had failed in that one essential way. I'd thought destroying the basement rosebush that fueled the malicious spirits who ran the school would free the students trapped here. From what I'd seen so far, my attempt had only left us trapped with greater horrors.

The guys moved toward the opening in the laundry room wall with lurching strides. I hung back, watching both Ryo and Elias carefully. When the younger guy swayed a little, I eased closer. "I can help—"

Ryo shook his head, his jaw tightening, and Elias fixed me with a firm stare that somehow managed to contain all of his teacherly authority even though he couldn't so much as walk on his own. "We'll manage. You can make sure the way is clear."

There obviously wasn't any point in arguing about it instead of getting a move on. As we passed the broken rosebush, I snatched the axe I'd used to destroy it off the ground. The tool might not have gotten me the victory I'd been hoping for, but its solid weight rested reassuringly in my hands. A metal blade probably couldn't do much against the transformed staff or the other apparitions emerging on campus, but it couldn't hurt to have a weapon at the ready.

Getting Elias through the hole in the wall took some maneuvering, but we managed without anyone collapsing. Making it up the stairs to the first floor was another trial. I edged along a few steps ahead of the guys, the axe braced in front of me, my muscles tensing at every thump and gasp that carried from above.

In the foyer, streaks of the thrumming energy that seemed to contain the staff's essences were still whipping this way and that. As I waited for the guys to climb the last few stairs, one bolt of light slammed into a girl's ankles as she darted by and sent her tumbling to her knees. I thought I could make out a faint murmur of laughter in the air.

I couldn't worry about her or anyone else right now. Keeping the three guys behind me safe was a big enough challenge on its own. I bit my lip, debating my options, but as unnerving as the scene in front of me was, what I'd seen outside had been even worse. And Elias wasn't in any shape to run. He needed to rest.

I made the best I could of the options available, all of which were bad. With a jerk of my hand, I directed the guys to the grand staircase in the middle of the foyer.

"Upstairs to the dorms. I don't know what all we're dealing with, but we can barricade ourselves in there against any physical threats for as long as we think we have to. Elias needs to get off his feet and recover."

If he even could recover more. If his rose didn't simply keep leaching his life away by the minute. I swallowed thickly.

None of the guys argued. By the time we'd made it to the second floor, my suggestion was starting to look not so bad after all. A few students lingered in the hall outside the classroom doors, but neither hostile spirits nor misty ghosts showed any sign of making their way this high up.

Maybe we'd be okay up here until whatever was going on across campus died down.

Assuming it did die down on its own.

We shuffled past the closed classrooms and up the stairs to the boys' dorm. The bedroom where Elias and I had cuddled on his bed just a few hours ago was empty. I grasped his arm as the other two lowered him onto the mattress. He flopped down with a ragged exhalation of relief, but it looked as if a little color had come back into his face. Maybe he was stabilizing?

Ryo dropped onto the edge of a neighboring bed. Jenson peered out the door, shut it, and dragged one of the other beds to block it from opening. I stayed on my feet, too keyed up to consider sitting.

Jenson leaned against the headboard of the bed he'd blocked the door with, crossing his arms. "What the hell is going on out there? What's going on with him?" He motioned briskly toward Elias.

"Everything went so crazy when you took down the bush that I couldn't make a whole lot of sense of it," Ryo put in.

I paced from one end of the room to the other. "I don't know exactly what happened. It seemed like when I chopped through the base of the bush, all the energy that was sustaining it—and I guess sustaining the teachers and the dean too—exploded. I think they leapt in and… absorbed that energy somehow? They dropped the physical bodies they've been using. I guess those adult bodies were always just a front for the spirits of the eight students from the portraits." I paused. "In the middle of it, I had another memory from way before—I saw the eight of them in the basement, cutting up their wrists. They meant to die, but they woke up some kind of dark power by making their suicides a sacrifice."

*Take our blood and theirs*, the boy who'd seemed to be the leader—Oscar Frederickson, who'd positioned himself as Roseborne's dean in the present day—had said. Who were the *theirs*? The students whose faces had been crossed out in the 1927 yearbook I'd found?

What had Oscar's eight done to them?

"Can this get any more fucked up?" Jenson muttered, in a tone that clearly said he doubted it. He couldn't state the sentiment outright. Roseborne laid a curse on all its students as a punishment for their past crimes, and Jenson's was that he couldn't speak the truth. At best, he could use only questions and commands to get his thoughts across.

Elias shifted on his bed and pushed himself upright. He swiped his hand over his face, which definitely looked less haggard than before, if still more strained than I'd have preferred. Good. If he was recovering, at least some of his weakening must have been because of the spirits' attack rather than anything permanent happening to his rose.

"The rosebush in the basement served *some* function," he said. "Do you think the staff—these spirits or whatever they are now—can really carry on like they did before?"

"I can't see Roseborne going back to having classes and all that," I said. "The spirits have dropped their facade now. Maybe they're just making the most of this last burst of power before it seeps out of them, and we'll get out of here once they fade away."

"Or maybe they're strong enough to hold onto that power even without the basement rosebush," Ryo said quietly. "There's still the bigger one outside."

"Yeah." I hugged myself. "And it's not just those spirits we have to deal with. I took a look outside—I think the roses on the wall are shriveling faster. That would be why you're feeling weak all of a sudden." I tipped my head to Elias. "Also… there was this haze coming off the bush, some of it gathering into the forms of people. Like ghosts. I don't know how they appeared or what they're here for, but I don't see how it can be anything good."

"Agreed," Elias said grimly.

Ryo got up to walk over to the bedroom window, a small square high on the far wall. It gave a view over the back of campus, dark now with the thickening dusk. He peered out and returned to us, frowning.

"I can't see much out there, but there's no action around back right now. I guess we can hole up in here and see if everything settles down by the morning. If it doesn't… then it'll be obvious we have to figure out another approach."

Jenson's mouth slanted at a wry angle. "Does anyone know techniques for banishing ghosts? If they *don't* take off on their own, I'm sure handling eight decades-old spirits plus all these new ones will be a real piece of cake." He made no effort to disguise his sarcasm.

I looked at the axe I'd left by Elias's bed, but I couldn't chop up a being that was made of light or mist.

"Not really my area of expertise," Elias said.

"We'll figure out something," I said, ignoring the sinking sensation in my chest. We *had* to figure out something… I just had no clue what or how.

In the momentary silence that settled between us, the door knob rattled. Jenson flinched, springing away from the bed-turned-barricade. He spun around to stare at the bedroom door like the rest of us were. My fingers itched to grip the handle of the axe.

"We're using this room," Elias called out. "Take one of the others."

The person on the other side didn't answer. The knob clicked again, and the door jarred against the bed. The hairs on the back of my neck stood on end. I leapt forward instinctively to grasp the bed frame, to ensure it stayed in place—and a filmy figure slid straight through the solid wood of the door.

Narrowed eyes regarded me from a sour face with a nub of a chin. Richie. My pulse hitched, my feet freezing in place for one fatal second. The ghostly image of the guy I'd once watched beaten into a coma flung himself across the bed and dug his translucent hands into my chest.

# CHAPTER TWO

*Trix*

The dorm bedroom around me and the ghostly figure in front of me fell away. *I* seemed to fall —plummeting a long, long way into blurred depths with nothing to grasp hold of, my stomach dropping even faster. Then I jarred to a stop. My feet smacked against rain-glossed concrete in a narrow alley beside an apartment building.

Damp air and the hazy glow of distant streetlamps seeped through darkness that closed around me. A faintly rancid scent reached my nose from a dumpster farther down the alley. My heart skipped a beat. I hadn't been standing exactly here when I'd been in this place in reality—this wasn't the angle of my memories—but I knew exactly where I was.

It wasn't hard to guess why that spectral impression of Richie would have brought me here.

The second that thought passed through my head, footsteps pounded across the concrete toward me. I pressed myself flat against the brick wall, the rough texture prickling against my skin through my shirt. It all felt so *real*. But it couldn't be, because everything playing out around me had already happened a year ago.

Richie dashed into view, his dark hair flopping lank across his eyes, which were wide with panic. Cade barreled after him, just a couple of steps behind. My foster brother caught Richie by the wrist and hauled back so hard that Richie's feet tangled under him. The other guy would have fallen if Cade hadn't wrenched him back into balance. Richie let out a hiss of pain.

"I don't know what you're going on about, you maniac," he snapped, flailing to try to free himself from Cade's grasp at the same time. "I didn't even talk to Sylvie the other night. Why the hell would I bother? Just because I thought she was a bitch doesn't mean—"

Cade slammed his fist into Richie's face, cutting off the rest of that sentence. I flinched at the crunch of the smaller guy's nose breaking. My brother's narrow face was hard with anger, his light gray eyes flashing, the wiry muscle that filled out his frame coiled for another blow.

"I know you sent her that message," he said, his voice as harsh as his expression. "Who the hell else would have? Who the hell else would have been talking shit about her less than a week after she *died*?"

He swung again, clocking Richie in the jaw. Richie tried to shove him back with one hand while pawing at his bleeding nose with the other. My breath stayed locked in my throat, my chest aching for air.

This was when, in the real past, I'd come running after Cade and witnessed the rest of the fight. He'd been driving us home and parked with a screech at seeing Richie heading along the sidewalk. I hadn't known—I hadn't really thought he'd go anywhere near this far—

But I knew now. This fight, if you could call it that when Richie barely landed a single blow on Cade in return, ended with the guy battered and unconscious in this alley and then in a coma for weeks afterward.

I couldn't watch it play out all over again. Last time I'd stayed cringing in the shadows, knowing the only thing I could say that might end the beating was the last thing I wanted to admit. I'd been willing to let this guy take the fall for my crime. Even if Richie had been a jerk to me too over the years, even if he'd said crap about Sylvie, he didn't deserve this.

In the past several days, I'd found the courage to confess to the real Cade; I'd confessed to Ryo, Jenson, and Elias. I was stronger now.

I pushed myself away from the wall toward Cade and grabbed his shoulder. "Stop! Richie didn't hurt Sylvie. He didn't set anything up. It wasn't him."

My foster brother shoved the other guy to the ground and spun, his chest heaving. "What the fuck are you talking about, Trix?"

His hands were still fisted, the knuckles splotchy, white marked by smears of blood. His eyes practically blazed with a silvery fire. My back stiffened automatically.

Cade had never hurt *me*, not really. Not the way he'd laid into Richie. But in that moment as my pulse stuttered in my chest, I couldn't deny that there was another reason I'd hesitated to intervene.

I'd been afraid of him—not just of his disgust but of his rage, that he might turn on me this time. It wasn't normal, was it, to be terrified that one of those fists might swing at my face if I said the wrong thing? It wasn't normal that Cade had chased after a guy and beaten him into a pulp while he barely defended himself. Cade hadn't even had solid proof that Richie had anything to do with Sylvie's death.

Maybe Roseborne's spirits turning him into a literal beast as his punishment had been a little fitting after all.

Feeling the heat of his body and the flexing of his shoulder muscles beneath my fingers, the dank alley smells filling my nose and Richie's groan vivid in my ears, I had trouble remembering that none of this was real. Or at least, it wasn't happening now. He couldn't *really* hurt me in this memory brought to life... could he?

Pain twined through my chest with that question. How had we gotten to the point where I was this scared of the guy I'd counted on for so much, even in a conjured impression of the past? Whatever else Cade had done, he'd protected me plenty too. I'd built my whole life around the future we'd meant to forge together as friends, roommates, and as close to siblings as two people who didn't share blood could be. He'd made mistakes, and he'd pushed me in ways he shouldn't have, but he was still the brother who'd taken me under his wing when I had no one.

Without the vehemence he brought to both his anger and his affection, would he even have been able to keep us together all this time, stepped in to shield me when I'd needed it, and convinced our last set of foster parents to let us stay on after we'd aged out of the system? I'd loved the boldness in him even if it'd made me nervous sometimes. He just felt so much and so strongly that sometimes he overwhelmed the people around him, probably without even realizing it.

Holding on to that faith, I barreled onward with my confession. "I know Richie didn't do it because it was me. I sent Sylvie that text. I wanted to freak her out—it was just supposed to be a prank—it was stupid. I never meant for her to get hurt the way she did. If I could take it back, I would. But if you're going to be angry at anyone, it should be me. You can't take it out on him."

Richie was staggering to his feet. He shot me a disbelieving but maybe slightly grateful glance and half loped, half limped back toward the street. Cade just stared at me.

"No." He shook his head, slowly and then more sharply. "Why are you trying to defend him? He deserves all the hell I can rain down on him. I know you're tougher than this, Trix. Don't let me down by getting all soft."

He moved to charge after Richie, and I clutched his shoulder, grasping his arm with my other hand at the same time.

"I swear to you, I'm telling the truth. I wouldn't throw

myself under the bus for Richie just for the hell of it. I mean it." Maybe I had to tell a little more truth before it would sink in. "I was jealous of her because you were spending so much time with her, because it seemed like she mattered more to you than I did. That doesn't make what I did okay—it's still awful—but that's why I wanted to freak her out."

Cade swung back around, his expression even wilder than before. I couldn't stop myself from wincing at the betrayal etched on his face. "Don't do this, Trix. Don't tell me this shit. I don't *want* you to mean it."

Some part of me wanted to erase the revulsion I'd provoked, to pretend I'd made it all up. Richie had gotten a good head start by now. I'd saved him. Why should I have to face any more of this imaginary Cade's reaction when the real one had already told me he understood?

Because it didn't matter what anyone else said. *I* knew I'd fucked up. Until I owned that fact all the way through, how could I really say I was sorry for it?

The words came out quiet and strained but clear. "I wish I didn't mean it either. It *is* true, though. You can't blame anyone but me. So… do whatever you need to do."

I let go of him and stepped back, my arms falling to my sides. My spine went rigid in anticipation of his possible retaliation. Cade turned all the way to face me, his jaw working. I could have run—my muscles twitched with the urge to—but I held my ground.

I blinked, and that ground dissolved beneath my feet, the darkness and the brick walls wisping away too. The world spun around me in a blur so dizzying my guts flipped over. Then I was stumbling forward onto the bed that was pushed in front of the dorm bedroom door, banging my shins against the frame. My fingers curled into the thin blanket.

"Trix!" Ryo was at my side in an instant. His arm slid around me as my own arms wobbled in their attempt to hold me up. "Are you okay? What did that thing do to you?"

My voice came out hoarse. "I ended up in—sort of a vision. A memory. A time when I screwed him over—the guy who came for me." I wet my lips, gradually regaining control over my trembling body. "I did better by him this time. I guess that's why I was able to come out."

The ghost-like figure of Richie that had sunk its hands into my chest had vanished. For good or just for the moment? It'd come straight through the door. That meant we weren't safe here. I wasn't sure we'd be any safer anywhere else on campus, but the makeshift barricade I was bracing myself against felt abruptly flimsy.

"I can't get it off him," Elias muttered somewhere behind me. The tension in his voice made my nerves jump. I pushed myself upright and swiveled around.

While I'd been gripped by Richie's "ghost," another filmy figure had come calling. Jenson lay sprawled on the floor between the beds, the translucent form of a teenaged girl leaning over him. Her hands had plunged into his chest the way Richie had done to me. Jenson's eyes were closed, his eyelids twitching, his mouth pressed into a tight line.

Elias had pushed himself to the edge of his bed and

was swiping at the ghostly figure. His hands passed right through her without making her so much as quiver. Ryo gave me a quick sideways hug and went to join him, but his attempt to catch hold of her was just as futile.

"How long has she had him?" I asked, stepping toward them with a stutter of my pulse. "How long was *I* out of it?"

"You were stuck there fifteen minutes, maybe twenty?" Ryo made a grimace as another grab at the girl failed. "We were all trying to get it off of you, and this one came seeping in and went straight for Jenson."

"He looked like he recognized her," Elias said grimly.

Considering my experience, that wasn't surprising. I was going to guess that all the apparitions wandering the school were people from our pasts—people we'd rather not have to face. What was this girl making Jenson live through?

There might be more coming for Elias and Ryo—the image of Sylvie I'd seen by the gate might be coming up here for me. It was too much of a coincidence to think these two had just happened to end up encountering us while none that weren't associated with us had ventured this far. They knew how to track us down.

"They're drawn to us somehow," I said. "Staying here isn't going to protect us." Maybe if we simply kept on the move—but we couldn't move Jenson anywhere while he was trapped by this thing, and no way in hell was I abandoning any of my guys.

I sucked in a breath, a tickle of the eerie energy that had flowed through me when I'd broken the basement wall rising up again. The ghostly figures were part of Roseborne's power, and so was I, thanks to my connection to Winston Baker. I hadn't been able to break out of Richie's hold without playing the game the vision had seemed to demand, but maybe I'd be able to challenge the others.

"Let me see what I can do," I said, waving Ryo to the side.

He moved and watched me with obvious concern. I willed the sense of power inside me into my hands. When I pushed them into the filmy impression of a girl, a chill tingled over my skin.

She didn't react any more than she had for the guys— but a sudden spiraling sensation washed over me, as if I were standing on the verge of a steep cliff, the wind buffeting me nearly to the point of toppling over the edge.

Jenson was down there. Down in the abyss of whatever memory this girl had stirred up. And I was struck by the certainty that I could follow him if I chose to.

I glanced at the other two. "I'm going to try to help him get out," I said, and shoved my hands deeper, throwing myself into the dizzying momentum, wherever it would lead.

# CHAPTER THREE

*Jenson*

Three years after graduating, I hadn't expected to ever find myself back at my old high school. Somehow, after the second spectral being to pass through the bedroom door had flung itself at me, here I was, standing in stark early spring sunlight by the equipment shed at the edge of the field, a lit cigarette poised between my fingers. The sharp nicotine scent prickled into my nose. On the opposite side of the squat concrete building, shouts rang out from an impromptu lunchtime football match.

This was where I'd always slipped off to when I'd taken a smoke break. The butts littering the patchy grass showed I was far from the only one. I didn't even like cigarettes all that much—I generally inhaled as little of the smoke as possible—but they added to the rebellious mystique I'd cultivated with my social circle here, and they made a convenient excuse to remove myself when I wanted a breather from the joking and jockeying for attention.

I wasn't alone now, though. Even if this day was pretty similar to plenty of other days when I'd stood here, the glimpse I'd gotten of the spirit-thing's face had told me what to prepare myself for. I'd barely registered my surroundings when Penny Bryant marched around the shed and came to a halt a few feet away.

It was weird, seeing her from the perspective of years later. When this moment had happened in reality, she'd been sixteen and I'd been seventeen, and pursuing her had felt totally normal. Looking at her now that I was twenty-one, I winced inwardly at the thought of seducing a girl who was basically a kid. Not that I was planning on coming on to her all over again.

She would have let me—seventeen year old me as I must have appeared on the outside in this dream or whatever the hell it was, anyway. I could see it even more clearly than I had back then, when I'd mostly been irritated by her interruption. Her dark blue eyes locked with mine in an accusing stare, framed by the smooth chestnut waves she always left in an artfully mussed state, but her body leaned just a little toward me. Her lips parted with a subtle flick of her tongue over them.

I'd hooked her right through to the gut, and she'd have taken sweet-talk over any kind of apology in an instant if I'd offered it.

"So, this is how it's going to be now?" she said in the arch voice she put on to pretend nothing really affected her. "You're going to act like you hardly even know me?"

In the actual past, I'd shrugged and said some bullshit about how she shouldn't have expected anything more, that we'd never been chummy when everyone was hanging out together, that it wasn't like we'd ever made anything official. As if I hadn't kept my flirtation on the down low specifically so that no one would realize I'd played her, and so she'd feel too awkward to confront me about it with anyone else looking on.

Taking up the quest of winning her over had been a risk as it was. I didn't normally dirty the waters within my main social circle. They were my proof that I was liked and a generally good guy, the basis of a reputation I could rely on if I wanted something from anyone else at school or on the fringes of our lives. But Penny...

She'd kept her distance from the moment she'd first started hanging out with our group. She'd rolled her eyes at my self-deprecating jokes and brushed me off if I tried to shoot the breeze with her. And the part of me that was bored and restless being at school couldn't resist a challenge that great.

It hadn't been all that hard, really. Most people were drawn to anything that let them feel special. I'd never made a move on any of the other girls in the group, but I started finding moments where I could offer a comment here or there apart from the others, where I could catch her eye and create an inside joke between just the two of us. Slowly but surely spooling out my fishing line, adding a compliment here, an apparently longing glance there, a subtle touch, all building up the idea that I was falling for her and couldn't stop myself. That she was the exception, the one girl I'd let my guard down for and show my softer side to.

Of course, I'd never really let down any guard. It'd all been another layer of the practiced persona I'd cultivated over the years. The whole time, I'd had the end goal in sight: the thrill of getting her under my thrall, of convincing her to make herself totally vulnerable to me.

Three days before this confrontation, she'd let me into her house, her bedroom, and her bed; I'd gotten her off and enjoyed myself plenty too, and then any interest I'd had in continuing the charade had shriveled up like the aging roses along Roseborne's wall. Since then, I hadn't talked to her one-on-one, hadn't answered her calls or even met her eyes other than in passing.

"What did you think was going to happen?" I asked her now, wondering if her answer would even mean anything. The beings that ran Roseborne College hadn't brought the real Penny here. Her response would just be whatever crap they or my own mind made up.

"You told me you wanted to be with me. That you couldn't stop thinking about me." She crossed her arms, hugging herself. "You said you'd wait as long as it'd take. So how can you just..." She trailed off as if she didn't know how to finish that question—or couldn't bear to.

Fresh irritation jabbed through my chest at her tone, both demanding and pleading. "I got to be with you. Funnily enough, that was all it took to stop thinking about you. I said I'd wait as long as it took, nothing about what I'd want after that."

Her flinch doused my annoyance with a splash of

guilt. It wasn't real, I reminded myself. And—what I'd just said was true, wasn't it?

Here in this weird blend of memory and dream, I'd been able to say something directly honest for the first time since I'd entered Roseborne. Both irritation and guilt fell away under a wave of exhilaration.

"No one forced you to buy into the big romantic picture I was painting," I went on with a lot more candor than I'd been willing to show back then, waving my hand at her. "You never questioned how I was keeping it just between us, or that you've never seen me get serious about *any* girl, or any of that. As soon as you were getting what *you* liked from me, none of the rest mattered to you. That part's on you."

Her chin came up defiantly. "You knew what you were doing. You tricked me and lied to me on purpose. You can't pretend that wasn't a shitty thing to do."

"Well, maybe I'm just a shitty person. You obviously thought I was when you first met me, or you wouldn't have given me the cold shoulder until I started buttering you up." I took a step toward her, flicking my cigarette aside. "I don't owe you anything. Just like no one's ever owed *me* anything. That's how the world works."

"Most people manage to make it through life without outright screwing people over just for the hell of it."

"Hey, you got your kicks too." I forced myself to smile, but the rush of speaking the truth had faded almost as quickly as it had come, leaving a dull queasiness.

I had been a shitty person. Shitty and selfish but at least somewhat satisfied, most of the time. Nothing about this past felt satisfying now, though. This was the road that had led me to Roseborne. This was the guy who wouldn't have recognized what was worthwhile in Trix.

I could barely believe Trix had given me a chance now —I sure as hell wouldn't have gotten one from her back then. She'd have laughed in my face, and I'd have told myself she was a bitch. I already knew I didn't want to fall into those patterns all over again.

But why should I have to justify myself to this mirage the school had created like a more vivid form of our counseling sessions?

"None of us mean anything to you, then?" Penny shot back at me. "We're just puppets for your amusement? Don't you care about *anyone* other than yourself?"

"I don't care about anyone who's so wrapped up in *themselves* that they can be strung along that easily. What makes you so special that you should get a free pass? If you want to be around people who actually care about you, make sure they're really acting like they do."

The last words had just fallen from my lips when I realized we were no longer alone in the space behind the equipment shed. My head jerked to the side.

Trix was poised on the sidewalk at the edge of the school field, her artificially orange hair swaying bright in the breeze and her brow knit. My throat constricted. How long had she been standing there listening? Although— was this just some new facet to the college's tortures, nothing to do with the actual girl?

Any hope I might have had that this wasn't really the girl I'd fallen for vanished a second later. "I managed to follow you in," she said, her gaze flicking between me and Penny. "It seems like the 'ghosts' that are coming after us are bringing us back to past mistakes. She's one of the people you lied to?"

"I didn't exactly *lie*," I said. I'd just said things that would sound like they meant a whole lot more than I actually intended. Maybe I'd exaggerated too. Fuck, I didn't want Trix seeing the fallout firsthand. She'd already had more than enough experience with what a prick I could be.

"Who the hell is she?" Penny broke in, her face flushing red. Apparently this "memory" could adapt to even as drastic a change as an entirely new person in the mix.

"None of your business," I told her. "You don't matter. You're not even real."

She blinked harder as if she were on the verge of tears.

"I don't think you're going to get out of the vision talking like that," Trix said quietly. "I couldn't leave mine until I admitted how I'd screwed up."

"It was four years ago," I protested. "A month out of her life. She wanted it too. I didn't force her to do anything." But saying those words to Trix only intensified my nausea. "Okay. I was a selfish bastard. I wouldn't do it again. But I can't help what happened back then."

That admission obviously wasn't good enough for this version of Penny. Her hands balled at her sides, and for a second I thought she might punch me. "You broke my heart, you asshole."

*I never asked for your heart*, I wanted to say, but I knew

how much of a lie that was. I might not have requested that depth of affection in so many words, but I'd hinted and nudged and led her down the path.

"That wasn't the point," I said instead. "It was just a— a side effect. I wasn't out to hurt you."

"But you knew it probably would hurt me, and you cared more about getting laid whatever way you could."

As if she ever would have looked twice at me if I really had opened up, shown her the guy underneath the front— father in jail, mom swallowed up by depression, not a cent between any of us that we'd gotten honestly, nothing to offer but some charm and quick wits. She wouldn't have just brushed me off but run in the opposite direction.

"You acted like you were better than me," I said.

"And that meant you had to bring me down?"

"No. Well. I just—"

I was only screwing this up more. I looked to Trix again, my shoulders tensed against a cringe. Her jaw was tight, the muscles in her slim arms taut. Like when she'd told us the story of her complicated relationship with Cade a few hours ago, forcing out the words like rough pebbles from her mouth.

The memory punched a hole through the center of me. I'd been silently raging at him with every admission she'd made. How *dare* he twist the love and loyalty that shone through her for him, manipulating her and making her dance to his tune no matter how it fucked her up?

But I'd treated Penny the same way, hadn't I? Maybe it wasn't as bad because there wasn't the same history there, and I didn't owe her as much… but I'd still preyed on her emotions in exactly the way I hated Cade for doing to Trix.

Whoever Penny was with now, he probably hated me exactly the same way, if she'd ever told him about me. In that moment, I hated me too.

"You just what?" Penny spat out.

I turned back toward her, and the words I hadn't been able to find earlier seared up my throat. "I shouldn't make any more excuses. I was an asshole to you, yeah, and you didn't deserve that. I'm sorry. I don't know what else to tell you. I can't make it better—I can only say I regret ever messing with your emotions. *No one* deserves that."

Penny faltered. Her posture slumped a little, and the anger fled her voice. "So where does that leave us?"

I groped for more truth—not satisfying at all this time, but possibly necessary. "It leaves me doing my best to figure out how to avoid being an asshole from here on, and you—hopefully you found someone to be with who means everything he says to you. I really am sorry."

I was. The apology rasped in my throat. The fact that it was genuine must have been audible, because Penny paused and then nodded. She still looked upset, but she walked away with her head held a little higher. No sense of victory rose up inside me.

Trix came over to me, resting her hand on my arm tentatively. I had the impulse to jerk it away. How could she want to offer any affection after the shitshow she'd just watched?

"Now you know how I ended up at Roseborne," I said,

keeping my tone as flat as possible. "Just multiply that by a hundred or so."

"Why?" Trix asked. A single syllable that held a massive weight.

"I don't know. It was the only way I knew how to be. All I saw from my parents, growing up."

"Your parents?"

"Yeah. My family life was… complicated." I set my hand over hers, running my thumb over her knuckles, reveling in the fact that she was here at all, that she'd come for me, that I'd been enough of something other than an asshole for her to think I was worth the effort. I could tell her this, what I'd never laid out for anyone before. I owed her even more than I had that figment with Penny's face.

"My parents were con artists," I said. "As far as I know, that's all they ever were. They'd get by running whatever scams they could until a place got too hot, and then we'd move on again. They started teaching me how to play a role in the cons from before I can even remember. Then, when I was nine, my dad got caught and put away, and my mom fell apart… so I did what I could to get by, keep myself fed and clothed and get whatever else I wanted."

The taut anxiety of those first several months before I'd gotten into a groove and built up more confidence echoed through me, knotting my innards. The pinch of hunger and the hollowness of our apartment where Mom had lain for days on end in the bedroom had driven me through my uncertainties. I'd survived it the best way I'd known how. That didn't mean I'd had no choices, though, then or later. I'd known right from wrong. I'd decided by easy and familiar vs. hard and scary instead.

I swiped my hand over my mouth. "I can't put all the blame on my childhood, though. I know at the end of the day the only person it comes down to is me. I'm still working on sorting myself out, as I'm sure you've been able to tell. But I do— Thank you, for coming and—"

Before I could finish that sentence, a spasm wrenched my body. Darkness washed through my mind, and then I was lying on my back on a wooden floor, three worried faces staring down at me.

Elias's dorm bedroom. I was back. I dragged in a breath of rose-scented air and shoved myself into a sitting position.

Trix was watching me—the completely real Trix, crouched by my knees. Was her expression a little warier than it'd been before? The scene she witnessed had to still be sinking in.

"Do you feel okay?" she asked carefully.

*No. Not at all.* I felt like throwing myself out the goddamned window. Of course, all I could do now was lie.

"It wasn't so bad," I said, pushing my mouth into a wry smile. I wanted to get out of here, away from her, before she could think any more about the bastard I'd been. What could I do that a bastard wouldn't when the whole campus was going to hell?

"This room obviously isn't safe," Ryo said. "We were coming up with another plan."

There. That was perfect. I scrambled onto my feet. "How's this for a plan? Stay here, rest up, and let Trix join forces with you against any more of those things that get in here. Let me go scout around campus and see which part is the most clear. Any objections?"

"Going off by yourself doesn't seem like the smartest idea," Elias said from where he was sitting on the edge of his bed. His hands were still braced against the mattress beside him as if it took some effort for him to keep his posture straight.

I fixed him with a pointed look. "Who's the least affected if the roses are dying faster? Haven't I been here by far the least time out of the three of us? Do you really think you'd help more than slow me down?"

"I can—" Trix started.

I was already shaking my head as I stepped toward the bed I'd shoved in front of the door. "Hold the fort. Who could protect those old-timers better than you? Give me a chance to see what news I can bring back."

Here was hoping I could come up with something more concrete than charm and wits to get us out of this hellhole.

# CHAPTER FOUR

*Trix*

"Jenson, hold on," I started, but he waved me off as he hustled out the door. I guessed nothing alarming lurked on the other side right now, because the only sound that followed was the thump of him shutting the door firmly behind him. The attitude he'd had as he'd left the dorm bedroom— defiant to any argument but with an almost frantic vibe that gave the impression he was fleeing from us—left my stomach knotted.

Why would he think he needed to get away from us—from *me*? Was it something about the scene I'd witnessed, the one the ghostly girl had provoked in his mind? Imagining how he'd played with her emotions hadn't been fun, but I'd seen enough in the present to know Jenson had grown beyond that selfishness. He'd put my safety and happiness ahead of his own more than once. Hell, he was doing that just now by leaving to try to find all of us better shelter.

Confronting her hadn't been easy for him, though. The defensiveness had been written all through his posture from the moment I'd arrived, before he'd even noticed me. If I hadn't been able to intervene... How would these spirits Roseborne had unleashed punish him—or any of us —if we failed to make up for our past sins as quickly and thoroughly as they'd like?

Jenson had only been at the school for a year, which made him less susceptible to the roses' aging, sure, but also meant he hadn't had as much time to come to terms with who he'd been. From what he'd said, conning people had been the only way of life he'd really known. Was he in a position to overcome all that at this exact instant? Ryo and Elias had been through far more of the confessions and brow-beating that the staff had used to force the students to confront their supposed sins. Jenson might actually be the *most* at risk out of all of us.

Ryo moved to the bed that had been blocking the door but stopped there with his lithe hand gripping the headboard. "I guess there isn't much point in trying to block the entrance when those things can walk through walls, is there?"

"Better put it back by the wall where it's supposed to be," Elias said, shifting on his bed. He did look steadier, but not back to the authoritative strength that usually emanated from him. "We don't want anything in the way of the door if we need to make a quick exit."

"Do you figure we can outrun them?"

I thought about the ghostly figures I'd seen on the lawn outside. "They didn't seem to move that fast… but maybe they can if their target is in sight." My imagined view shifted across campus to the dark stretch of the southern woods. The tension in my stomach deepened.

Cade was prowling through those woods—in his cursed beast form, which he'd be stuck in until half past midnight. What ghosts would be chasing him? Would being encased in the body of a monster make him less or more susceptible to their pursuit?

The memory of him furious and denying in the mirage of the alley contrasted with so many other moments recently and across our history. He'd been so apologetic the last time I'd seen him, so concerned, so focused on showing he was there for me. But some of that concern had been directed at pushing me away from the three guys he'd known I was getting closer with. And before that, for all the times he'd stood by me, reassured me, protected me, there were also the times he'd cajoled and guilted me in ways I hadn't fully recognized until I gave in to his desires…

I hadn't talked to him since I'd started to acknowledge how he'd twisted our relationship into something more about control and domination than love. It was hard to convince myself of how thoroughly he'd gotten me wrapped around his finger—would he recognize how screwed-up things had become if I confronted him about it? We'd both been through a lot of crap together, but that just made it more difficult to admit that some of the crap had been of our own making.

I glanced at Elias. He'd shared a painful element of his past to help me see how my foster brother's behavior had warped my reactions. I'd just admitted to both him and Ryo that I'd let Cade persuade me into shifting our bond from siblings to lovers despite my reluctance. Neither of them were likely to be enthusiastic about what I was going to say.

"I think I should check on Cade," I said. "He's on his own out there—no one else will even think to try to help him. I can't just abandon him, no matter what else I need to hash out with him. But I don't want—I'm not trying to abandon *you*."

Elias's expression softened. He reached to give my hand a quick squeeze. "Of course you're thinking of him too. He's your brother. I'm feeling a lot better than I was before. Why don't you see if you can convince him to come back here so we can all defend ourselves together? I don't think there's anything preventing him from leaving the woods."

My body balked instinctively at the idea of bringing together Cade and the guys he'd disparaged more than once, but I resisted that reaction. Whatever reasons he had for disliking them, surviving this fresh horror mattered more. We'd all be safer together.

If I was being honest with myself, *I'd* feel more secure around him if I had other people there to remind me he wasn't the only person who cared about me. To keep me from the desperate spiraling sensation that gripped me when he made it seem I might lose even him. Nothing good happened when that panic came over me.

I just had to get him here in the first place. Easier said than done.

"We'll be fine," Ryo agreed. "You go see what you can do for him. Unless—we could come with you…"

I shook my head at the question in his voice. I wasn't sure how Cade would react to seeing me with any other guy right now. Better to approach him on my own and work up to the trickier parts.

"I'll be back as fast as I can. If any more of those ghost things come around—as far as I can tell, they shouldn't hurt you, at least not right away. They just take you into a memory of something you did wrong. Your best bet if that happens is to focus on making amends however you can. That seems to be what they're looking for."

Ryo nodded, a shadow crossing his face as he must have pictured the scenarios he might face. I headed out before I had to feel any guiltier about taking off on them. The sooner I made it back, the better the chances that I'd be here before their past very literally caught up with them.

The hallway outside was dim and quiet other than muffled murmurs carrying from behind a couple of the other bedroom doors. A few of our fellow students had obviously hidden away up here, not that it was likely to do them any more good than it had us. I slipped past those rooms and down the stairs.

A few ghostly figures were drifting around on the second floor now, none of them people I recognized. As I dodged them, a girl dashed past me into one of the classrooms. A filmy presence glided along after her. I had the feeling she was going to have to face that figure sooner rather than later.

As I reached the mansion's front door, I picked up my pace. I didn't know how many other ghosts might be wandering, waiting for me, but Sylvie was definitely out there somewhere. Without even glancing toward the gate in case she was still nearby and my attention caught hers, I hurried across the lawn toward the woods.

A few other students had come this way and fallen before they'd reached the trees. A couple of the bodies sprawled under the faint glow of one of those ghostly presences. Over by the empty swimming pool, where I'd made my failed attempt at starting a vegetable garden to spite the school's love of destruction, one dark shape lay on its own. Fainted because of the shriveling of their rose, or left in that state when they hadn't passed whatever test an apparition had inflicted on them? Were they even still alive?

A lump crawled up my throat, but I jogged onward. I already had enough people to worry about saving without taking a detour along the way. It wasn't as if I could do anything for that poor soul no matter what they were suffering from.

I plunged into the woods, not bothering to worry about the twigs crackling under my feet. "Cade?" I called out. "Cade!" It hadn't been clear whether my brother could recognize me or my voice while he was in his beastly form, but I had to try whatever I could. There was a lot of forest to cover if I wanted to find him.

Late at night, he normally stuck to the deeper woods,

far beyond any light or noise from the rest of campus. The cool spring breeze licked over my cheeks as I hurried onward. I kept my ears pricked for any sound of movement in the forest around me, but I didn't hear anything that sounded large enough to be Cade's beast.

The minutes slipped by me with the thump of my heart. It felt like I'd been searching forever when my eyes caught on a hazy spot of light in the distance. Hustling toward it, I braced myself for whatever might await me.

Slumped on its side against a tree trunk lay a dark furry body: big as a bear with a wolf's muzzle, lips lined with curving teeth that interlocked in a terrifying fashion. I'd only seen Cade's monstrous form once before—it hadn't gotten any more pleasant. And now it was lit with an eerie light seeping from the ghostly man that leaned over the beast. Even out here in the forest, even though he was looking far more animal than human, the school's new spirits had tracked him down.

Who knew how long Cade had been grappling with this apparition—or how much longer he'd have before he met a worse fate?

I didn't let myself think, just stepped forward and shoved my hands into the ghost's back. My fingers clenched at the tingling that spread over them. I threw my consciousness forward into the connection between the ghost and my transformed brother.

The impression of falling didn't get any pleasanter with practice. I tumbled down through the vague darkness and slammed to a stop on a thinly carpeted floor. It was the floor of a living room in a house I didn't recognize, with a fraying flower-print couch by one wall, a tiny flat screen TV across from it, and a scratched up dining table filling the far end of the room. The smell of stale potato chips lingered in the air.

Cade stood in the middle of all that, his hands clenched and his muscles flexing, so close to how he'd looked in my memory of the alley with Richie that my pulse stuttered. The man I'd seen in the ghost that'd come for him kneeled hunched on the carpet in front of my brother, his graying hair and mustache drooping as much as his shoulders were. A red blotch marked his cheek— where Cade had already hit him?

"It's okay," the man said in a ragged voice. "You have no idea how sorry I am. I've been carrying around the guilt for almost twelve years. I know I should have done so much better by you. I was a wretched excuse for a father. Do what you have to do—I don't blame you at all."

A strangled sound of frustration worked from Cade's throat. "You don't get to apologize," he snapped. "You can't make it better. I was just a little kid, and you treated me like a punching bag."

This was his birth father, I realized. The memory didn't make any sense to me, though. Almost twelve years, his dad had said—but Cade had told me he'd been taken from his birth family and placed in foster care when he was six. That was fourteen years ago, and as far as I'd been aware, he hadn't seen his parents since then.

But apparently he had. Apparently he'd tracked down his dad when he was around eighteen without telling even me about it. Tracked him down and… gotten into a fist-fight with him?

Although this didn't look like an equal fight any more than his beating of Richie had. If anything, this was worse. His dad wasn't even trying to get away.

"I know," the slumped man said now. "So if you need to do this, go right ahead. Lord knows I deserve it."

Cade's stance wavered. He looked as if he might have drawn back. Then, quick as lightning, he punched his dad across the temple so hard his dad's head jerked to the side, body swaying.

"You fucked up my entire life, you asshole," Cade gritted out through clenched teeth. He drove his knee into the older man's jaw, and then slammed both hands down on the side of his head so his dad collapsed right onto the floor. "Don't try to tell me what's okay. Don't act like you're such a fucking martyr. Stop hiding behind this pathetic act and show me the shithead I know you are!"

As he jammed his foot into his dad's ribs, I sprang forward. I couldn't stand to watch any longer. I had no idea how well this echoed what had happened in the past, but presumably it hadn't gone *better* than this. And Cade was being sucked into the same anger that must have gripped him back then.

I flinched as I grasped his arm, wanting to help him, wary of how he'd react to me at the same time. "Cade. Stop. It's not real. You've got to stop!"

Cade stumbled backward, staring at me. "Trix? What the hell—how are you here? You weren't here." Some of the color drained from his face, leaving it pale between the ruddy splotches of anger.

"It's me—really me," I said. "It turns out I can step into these visions even when they're gripping other people. I came so I can help you. Everything on campus has gone crazy. And I mean even more so than usual."

He blinked, his jaw working. "I— You— What am I supposed to do with this prick?" He swung his arm toward his dad, who was still lying crumpled on the floor in a daze, blood trickling from the corner of his mouth. Cade's chest heaved with strained breaths. "I guess I should have laid into him even harder the first time."

"No." I squeezed his arm. "Roseborne is trying to make us face up to our mistakes. The reasons we ended up here. For you..."

For him, it was clearly that anger. The anger I hadn't known he'd let loose to this extent. I'd thought his attack on Richie in the alley had been an anomaly. But he hadn't run into his dad in his dad's own house by accident. He'd come here—he'd *planned* to beat him up?

"He deserved this," Cade said, as if he could tell where my thoughts had led me. "The bastard even said it himself."

"He doesn't deserve anything from you," I said. "Not even your anger. You should just cut him out completely, forget about him."

"You don't know—the nightmares I still had, for years and years—and the social workers told him, they told him and Mom that they'd have to take me away if the two of them didn't shape up, and he didn't care, he didn't even *try…*"

Cade swiped his hand over his face, his expression so fraught it wrenched at my heart. I tugged him to me, wrapping my arms around him. A shudder passed through him. After a moment, he returned the hug tightly.

An uneasy itch ran over my skin at the thought of the ways the gesture of affection could be misinterpreted, of how he'd built off of similar moments in the past, but right now, my brother needed me. I could focus on that. On all the moments when his embrace hadn't meant anything more than getting *me* through some horrible event. We stood by each other. That was what we did, more than anything else.

"Let go of that anger as much as you can," I said. "That's the only way you'll get out of this place. Help him up, show that you can manage that without hurting him any more, and then walk away. I think that's all it'll take."

"I don't want to help that asshole. Let him get his own self up."

"Cade…" I pulled back to look him in the eyes. "Is this really who you want to be? Someone who goes around beating people into a pulp?" That wasn't the guy I'd thought I'd known.

He gazed back at me, his mouth twisting. "You think *I* deserve what they did to me. Is that really all you see, after everything we've been through?"

"Of course not. But I don't think letting out this kind of rage is good for anyone, you included. Don't you trust me?"

"Don't *you* trust me?"

I swallowed hard. "This isn't really about that. I know more about what's going on right now. I can see the way out. Don't turn this into some kind of statement of loyalty or who loves who more. You *know* I love you. I can still think you're heading the wrong way."

Something shifted in his eyes like a scudding cloud. Maybe he could tell I was talking about more than just this specific moment. "Trix," he said, his voice even rougher than before, "you've got to believe me, I've *always* been looking out for you, no matter what else was going on—"

I stepped back before he could keep going. Those tendrils of guilt were already creeping through my chest with every word. I couldn't let him distract me, wrap me up in his intentions, like he had so many times before, whether he realized what he was doing or not.

"We're not getting into that right now," I said as calmly as I could manage. "You need to settle this with your dad so we can escape this vision before it turns into something worse."

"Trix—"

"Cade. We can talk about the rest later."

For a second, he all but glowered at me. But only for a second. Then he strode toward his dad and grabbed the guy's hand. With a yank that wasn't exactly gentle, he guided the older man to his feet.

"She's right," he said tersely. "I shouldn't have gone looking, shouldn't even care what you did to me after all this time. I don't need this kind of trouble. You live your life, and I'll live mine, as far as I can get from you."

Without waiting for his dad's response, he swiveled on his heel and stalked back to me. He motioned for me to follow him down the hall to the house's front door. The set of his shoulders suggested he'd only walked away under a sense of duress. I had to hope it'd be enough.

I grabbed his hand. "When we're back in the real world, come with me to the school building. I can help you if you get sucked into another of these visions, but it's easier if we're all together."

Cade's head snapped toward me. "Who the hell is this 'all'?"

A sense of resolve rose up inside me. "You were wrong," I said. "There are other people who care about me and stand beside me. It's not just you. If you really care about me and not only about keeping me on some kind of leash, you'll stand with all of us."

The last words were just falling from my mouth when the scene around us whirled away. I found myself stumbling on the forest floor a couple of feet from where Cade's beast was just lurching onto its feet.

We locked eyes through the darkness. I held out my hand, ignoring the abrupt racing of my heart. My brother was inside that beast, no matter how horrific it looked.

"Come with me," I said. "Please. Even like this."

The monster didn't move. Then it lunged at me with a gnash of its interlocking teeth, so close its rancid breath stung my cheek. A yelp I couldn't restrain hitched out of me.

I scrambled backward. The thing that was Cade and yet not slashed its claws across my foreleg, drawing an immediate searing pain through my skin. With a howl that reverberated through the forest and right down to my bones, it whipped around and charged off between the trees.

# CHAPTER FIVE

*Ryo*

It'd been easy enough to tell Trix she should go see if her brother needed help. Hanging around waiting for her to get back was a hell of a lot harder.

Thankfully, Elias appeared to feel the same way. I hadn't wanted to urge him to get moving or to leave him alone after the way he'd collapsed downstairs, but he'd recovered enough that after a few minutes, he pushed himself to his feet. He gripped the bed's headboard and then let it go to stand without support.

"We can't just sit here waiting for her and Jenson," he said. "There has to be something constructive we can do."

"Sounds good to me." I glanced toward the door Trix had slipped past. "Do you have any specific ideas?" I was man enough to admit that leadership skills came to him way more naturally than they did to me—and I'd happily follow that lead.

Elias frowned. "Maybe we should gather together more than just the four of us and Cade. We can't shield ourselves from these ghosts or whatever the school is sending at us, but with large enough numbers, we might be able to… distract them, or divert them?"

"Sounds worth a try." I motioned toward the door. "Should we see who we've got to work with?"

We went down the hall, Elias walking steadily if carefully, and knocked on the other bedroom doors. "We're meeting in the second floor hall in ten minutes," Elias told the guys who'd had the same idea of escaping up here as we had. "The things coming after us now, they can go right through walls. Hiding isn't going to protect us."

At one of the rooms, he didn't need to add that last part. The guy inside was braced rigid by the foot of his bed, staring at his fallen companion, who was slumped in the grips of a ghostly form. Even after witnessing the act twice before and with people I cared about more, the sight made my skin crawl.

"If he hasn't come out if it in ten minutes and you're okay with leaving him, come down and talk with us," Elias told the other guy. "We'll try to work out some ideas for making them back off even after they've got a hold on someone."

The guy nodded with a nervous purse of his lips, but he looked grateful just to know he wasn't alone. We'd all experienced plenty of awfulness here at Roseborne, but none of us could have predicted the turn the college had taken in the past hour.

When we'd reached the second floor, I stopped to peer out one of the small windows that overlooked the front of campus. More of the ghosts or whatever they were stood out with their pale glow against the growing darkness. The mist Trix had mentioned glowed too, still seeping off the rosebush along the wall. As I watched, another translucent figure and yet another formed from its haze.

They brought on memories of things we'd done wrong, Trix had said… Who exactly had that guy been who'd grabbed her? Or the girl who'd come at Jenson?

Who would I find myself facing first?

That question sent a shiver down my back. I tore my gaze away.

A few of the ghosts were roaming near the classrooms. One of them vanished right through a doorway—after its intended target? We really weren't safe anywhere unless we could come up with a working strategy for either dodging or repelling them.

"Should we check on the girls too?" I asked Elias.

He paused and then nodded. "I think they'll forgive the intrusion, considering the circumstances."

We tramped up the stairs on the other side of the building and repeated the same process we had in the male dorms. At first glance, the last room, at the end of the hall, appeared to be empty. Then a body stirred beneath the blankets on one of the beds. I recognized Violet Droz's billowy hair before her face turned to reveal the patchwork of raw scars that covered half of it. They looked even more stark than usual against the sallow shade the rest of her skin had turned.

"What's going on?" she asked, her voice not much more than a croak. I didn't remember her seeming at all weak before tonight. Her rose must be faltering fast like Elias's had—and unlike him, she hadn't been able to bounce back as well.

Did she have any idea at all what was happening outside this room?

"Things have gotten… stranger than usual," Elias said. "In a way that we suspect is putting us all in immediate danger."

Her eyes narrowed. "Trix did something crazy, didn't she?"

A jolt of defensiveness shot through me. "She was *trying* to get us out of here. And she might have gotten us a lot closer than we've ever been before."

Violet groaned and let her head fall back onto her pillow. "She should have just let me die, if that was where I was headed."

Let her die? What had Trix done for her? "What are you talking about?" I asked.

"She didn't tell you? I thought—I just wanted to stop this place from messing with me anymore. It's all connected to the roses… I cut mine. Meant to snip it right off, but it didn't quite work. Of course she had to find me and replant the damn thing."

From the slant of her mouth, I wasn't sure she really did regret getting Trix's help. That'd been a hell of a statement she'd tried to make. Obviously she'd been in a pretty bad state even before total chaos had descended on the campus.

"There are things like ghosts—people from our lives before Roseborne, wandering around," Elias said. "If one reaches you, it whisks you away somehow, into one of the bad times you experienced before." He glanced at me. Neither of us could fully explain what *we* hadn't yet experienced ourselves.

When I shrugged as a way of saying I didn't have anything to add, he turned back to Violet. "Apparently you have to make some kind of amends to get back out. But we're working on a plan for stopping the ghosts from getting to their targets in the first place. Are you strong enough to make it downstairs? We could bring some blankets so you could lie down on the floor there. You'd just be safer if you have people around to help."

Violet was silent for a long moment. Her gaze had gone distant. She shifted her limbs under the covers. "I don't know. Maybe… maybe if something like that is coming for me, I should have to face it."

Despite her snarky remarks about Trix, the thought of leaving anyone alone up here made my chest clench up. "We could carry you down, if you need that."

She grimaced. "No, thank you. If I feel up to it later… Don't worry about me. I'll look after myself."

"If you change your mind, give us a shout," Elias said.

Hopefully one of us would be close enough to hear.

By the time we made it back to the second floor, a small crowd was already gathering near the banister overlooking the grand staircase. Maybe a dozen of our fellow students circulated restlessly outside the classroom doors.

As we reached them, another of the ghostly wraiths came floating up the stairs. Someone at the back of the group inhaled sharply. They must have recognized the stern-looking woman.

Elias stepped forward to intercept the ghost. It glided around him as if it'd barely noticed he was there. It hadn't gone right through him, though.

"Whoever that one's after, stick close to the rest of us," I suggested, raising my voice to carry. "Everyone else, keep moving. Get in front of it, don't give it any openings."

The others murmured in unsettled tones. "I don't want that thing getting anywhere near *me*," someone said under their breath.

"They won't do anything to you if it's not you they're here for," Elias said, but that didn't ease the uneasy energy that hung in the air.

Most of the crowd did at least attempt to follow my idea. They shifted this way and that as the ghost approached—and she drifted between them even where people stood shoulder to shoulder, not seeming to touch them, just squeezing through some impossibly small space in an instant to appear on the other side.

Her target obviously realized we weren't going to offer much protection. He swore and took off, dashing around the bannister and then down the stairs the way the ghost had come. It swiveled and followed, skimming across the ground faster now.

"We're not enough to put them off on our own," I said to Elias. "What now?"

He was frowning. "They're connected to the rosebush outside somehow, aren't they? The mist is coming off of that, and they're forming from the mist. We didn't see any of them in the basement when we were down there. I wonder how they'd react to the other bush, the one that was holding all the staff's energy."

"The one Trix destroyed." Would they be drawn to it? Horrified by it? Any effect we could get at all might make a difference. "Let's find out."

"Try to stay calm and to do what you can to defend each other," Elias instructed the crowd with his teacherly air. "We'll be back soon with a plan that might make that easier."

I hustled after him as he strode down the stairs. The flashes of light we'd seen in the foyer on our way up had either faded away or traveled elsewhere. As we descended into the basement, a wary prickling ran down my spine, but nothing horrifying met us there. Well, nothing more horrifying than the dank, blood-stained room scattered with the crumbled bits of that eerie rosebush, which we'd seen before.

There weren't any ghosts lurking around down there, but then, there weren't any students around for them to have followed. Elias stooped and gathered handfuls of the broken brambles to shove into his suit pockets. I gazed over the mess in the flickering light. A glimmer of inspiration lit in my head: a picture of how this could come together. But we'd need more than a few scoops.

"Take your jacket right off," I said. "We can use it to carry a lot more that way."

Elias raised his eyebrows at me. "Are you sure we need a lot?"

I suspected he wasn't totally comfortable taking off any part of his suit. I'd never seen him in anything *other* than a suit even before he'd started teaching Roseborne's impossible math class. It was tied up in his sense of identity somehow.

I gestured to the mess on the floor. "Might as well bring as much as we can upstairs, right? Either it'll help somehow, in which case it'll be good to have plenty, or it won't do anything, in which case it won't hurt that we brought a bunch. This bush obviously isn't attracting the things, or some of them would have come down here."

"Fair enough." He balked a second longer and then peeled off the suit jacket. As soon as he laid it out on the floor, I started scooping up the brambles and tossing them onto the fabric. A thorny edge pricked my thumb; another scratched across my palm. I ignored the slivers of pain and kept adding to the heap.

More energy came into Elias's movements as he moved alongside me. Getting down to work had rejuvenated him at least a little more. *I* felt more energized, even without knowing whether this effort would accomplish anything.

I'd brought more light and hope into Trix's life by standing by her, even if those brighter emotions only shone dully inside me thanks to the college's curse. I'd started to see that I could make a difference for other students here too. Why wouldn't that also apply to the guys I'd ended up the most closely connected with?

I didn't want us to turn our mutual relationship with Trix into some kind of competition. It'd be better for all of us if we collaborated in every possible way rather than fighting each other, wouldn't it?

It hadn't taken long for us to heap all we could into the jacket. Elias bundled the edges over the brambles and lifted it.

"Are you good with that?" I asked him. "I can carry it."

He waved me off. "They're pretty light. I'm not an invalid."

"No, definitely not." I shot him a quick smile as we passed through the gap in the wall that Trix had managed to open up with her unexpected power. "You know, as messed up as this situation has gotten—even more messed up than it was before—I'm glad we can tackle it together. Roseborne spends a huge amount of time encouraging us to focus on our own flaws and everyone else's, doesn't it?"

"I suppose so," Elias said. "That seems to be the point."

"Both to punish us and to make sure we *don't* work together, I'd bet. But we've all got strengths too, even if this place wants us to forget that. We've got things we can contribute. And we can do a heck of a lot more when we join forces."

"Are you going somewhere with this?"

I didn't let his skeptical tone rankle me. "I'm just saying... Even with all the shit Roseborne has put us through, I can recognize what's good in you. You saw the potential benefits in gathering the students in greater numbers. You thought of seeing if we can use the bush. I'll do my best to pitch in too."

I couldn't tell if my words really sank in. As we tramped up the stairs, Elias didn't look particularly more confident or pleased than before. Well, I was glad I'd said it anyway. We spent enough time here being beat up or beating up ourselves emotionally. It was about time we shared some praise instead.

The crowd on the second floor had thinned some in our absence, but a few people had noticed our purposeful path through the foyer and followed us up, so I figured our numbers had about evened out overall.

"What's all that for?" someone demanded as Elias set down the jacket.

"We're about to find that out," he replied.

Quite literally. Another ghost was flitting up the staircase after us. I bent over to grab a couple of the bramble shards and tossed them at the thing.

The hazy figure flinched. The brambles that fell to the floor in front of it didn't stop it completely, but it wavered for a moment with a faint tremor through its glow before it dodged them. The hint of inspiration that had hit me in the basement flared up with renewed intensity.

"The art room," I said to Elias, and loped to the door without waiting to see if he agreed with my idea.

The door opened at my twist of the knob. I ducked inside and ran to the cabinet at the far end of the room where Professor Filch kept the canvases. As I grabbed several of the larger ones, a little taller and wider than my torso, Elias joined me.

"This doesn't seem like a good time to be painting pictures."

"That's not what we're doing with these." I tipped my head toward a few more stacked at the back of the cabinet. "Grab those other ones there."

I hurried back out and set the canvases on the floor. My fingers working faster than I'd pushed them in ages, I snatched up one broken bramble and another and poked the sharp edges into the fabric that was stretched across the wooden frame. By the time Elias had followed me back to the crowd, I'd constructed a ring of shattered rosebush around the edge of the canvas and dotted the white surface with several more twigs across the middle.

"Shields," I said by way of explanation, and hefted that one up by the frame. "If a bunch of us hold them, we might be able to keep the ghost-things away completely."

The muttering around us faded as our classmates looked on with interest. "What are you waiting for?" someone said. "Let's get more of them, then."

I dove back into the task, a few of the others taking canvases of their own and copying my initial pattern. I had no idea whether the specific shape I'd used made any difference, but it looked more shield-like, and maybe that was important.

Within a matter of minutes, we had seven of the makeshift shields. I grasped one, Elias another, and five volunteers took up the others. We formed a protective circle around the rest of the group.

Our activities seemed to have caught the attention of more of the wraiths. Two more were drifting through the hall, another climbing the stairs. As they approached, we moved closer together, Elias's shoulder brushing the wall beside him.

The ghosts might not have been intimidated by us standing together unequipped, but the bramble shields made them think twice. One spun away from us with a shudder. Its companion swung close but continued on in its wobbly arc rather than trying to push past us.

Someone behind me let out a laugh of relief. I couldn't help grinning at Elias when our eyes met. "Now we're getting somewhere."

Finally, an answering smile crossed his face. "Yeah," he said. "It looks that way. Good thinking."

"Couldn't have done it without your thinking first."

He looked as if he might have said something else, but as he opened his mouth, a ghost that must have been prowling through the classrooms glided through the wall right behind him, its hands grasping.

"Elias!" I said like a warning, not fast enough. Elias started to jerk around, and the wraith plunged its hands into his back.

# CHAPTER SIX

*Trix*

I stopped at the edge of the woods and knelt down to take a look at my calf in the moonlight. Cade's monstrous claws had sliced through my leggings. The edges of the slashes in the fabric had gone soppy with blood, my flesh raw red beneath. The initial razor-like sting of the wound had expanded into a dull throbbing that ran from my ankle to my knee. My throat constricted, taking in the damage.

Why had he attacked me like that? Because I'd told him I was sticking with the other guys? Because I'd resisted his attempt to direct the conversation and my emotions? Or maybe he hadn't been aware enough of any of that once he'd fallen back into beast form—maybe all that had lingered was whatever burst of anger our conversation and his confrontation with his dad had stirred up. I didn't even know if he'd realized who he was attacking.

There wasn't much I could do about the injury now. Back in the school, I could find a clean kitchen towel or something to wrap it with. Squaring my shoulders, I straightened up and set off across the lawn with a slight limp.

As I walked, I scanned the area around the school for Jenson's tall, slim frame. Was he still out here searching for a safer stronghold? He might have been caught by another ghost from his past. I didn't see any sign of him.

By now, he might have gone back to Elias and Ryo to make further plans. Whether Cade ended up joining us or not was up to my brother. I'd helped him, warned him, and offered all the support I could. As much as I hated to leave him behind, I needed to make sure the other people I'd come to care about here made it through the night—and whatever awaited us after.

A trail of glowing light whipped across the lawn ahead of me, scattering a small cluster of nervous students in its wake. I made out a glimpse of a boyish face and a burgundy school uniform within the glow before it swept back around toward a few other patches of light that were skimming along the outside of the school building. Apparently the former staff had gotten bored with harassing the students inside.

Did it look as if their energy had dwindled at all? As far as I could tell, they shone just as brightly as when they'd first absorbed the energy from the rosebush. How much were they controlling the other horrors happening around us?

My instinct was to give them a wide berth, but what

progress I'd made toward getting us free hadn't happened by avoiding conflict. Instead, I strode straight up to them, staying tensed to defend myself or make a run for it if I felt I needed to.

"You're not going to teach us much like this, are you?" I hollered at the glowing spots. They paused to hover above me like spotlights. "How much longer do you really think you can keep any of this up before you run out of juice?"

The four of them slunk down the building, and three more rippled across the grass to join the group. As they drew closer, it was easier to pick out the human features half-swallowed by the energy wrapped around them. The spirit boy who stopped directly in front of me, with messy black hair over deep-set eyes and a prominent nose, had once presented himself as the school's dean. From the faded memories I'd glimpsed of the school's distant past, he'd led this toxic group back then too.

I crossed my arms over my chest. "Hello, Dean Wainhouse. Or I guess I should just call you Oscar now."

The light around the boy's form twitched. His lips curled with a sneer. The figures flanking him were equally familiar from the portraits in the school hall, the photographs in the old yearbook I'd found, and those memories that weren't mine but those of the eighth of their number—Winston, the one who'd left. The one I was increasingly sure had been my great-grandfather.

At my right, the dark-haired girl with a flying bird necklace tucked under the collar of her shirt was Mildred Christoph—Professor Hubert in her college staff guise.

She was the only member of the group I thought I might have gotten through to at all, however much my conversations with her would matter now. She peered at me intently, her expression difficult to read. From the photographs she'd kept in her office, she'd had a particular interest in Winston. Did she know how connected to him I was?

Oscar's voice came out sounding younger but just as dry as it had in his dean persona, clear despite the haziness of the light around him. "You seem to think you know a lot, Miss Corbyn. We still hold the power here."

"Do you? If you could have held it all inside you to begin with, I'm not sure why you needed some monster of a rosebush in the basement."

"It was convenient to our ends. We're nothing if not adaptable."

Flickers of the fragmented memories I recognized as Winston's rather than my own passed through my head: Oscar standing at the front of an otherwise empty classroom, looking down his nose as he announced, *If we're going to do this, we need to be all in. You're either with us or you're the enemy. It's up to you.* Then Mildred and one of the other girls stalking across the lawn toward the pool ahead of me, the other girl swiping at a bloody nose. Mildred's shirt showed a damp blotch of a stain—tea or maybe coffee. *We'll show them. This school belongs to us just as much.*

"Isn't it about time you let go of old grudges?" I asked. "No one here now ever hurt any of you. Why don't you adapt to that? You've punished them plenty—you've *killed* masses of them. Isn't that enough? Let them out of here, and you can find something better to do with your time." The former staff might not be conjuring our ghosts, but I had no doubt that they decided whether the gate stayed locked.

"They're just like the miscreants who used to lord it over us back in the day," one of the other guys rasped out. "Only thinking about themselves, how they can get what *they* want, even better if they can stomp on someone else along the way. Everything they've been through here, they deserve."

"They won't *stop* deserving it until they're finished paying," Mildred added.

"From what I've seen, you were pretty awful to the people you hated back then too," I said.

Oscar shifted his stance, drawing himself up even taller. In that moment, a dark current flitted through the energy glowing around him like a waft of smoke. Something about its intensity and its snakelike motion sent a chill straight through my bones. The erratic pulse that radiated from him in that moment reminded me of the demented power I'd felt from the basement rosebush.

"We paid them back only a small portion of the abuse they heaped on us," he said. "They took and took and took from us, and we only stole back what we were owed. We paid to make this school ours, a thousand times over."

Another memory: out by the gazebo in the sparser northern woods, Oscar and a few of the others, shadows stretching with the descending evening. *Is it even going to work?* I—or rather, Winston—asked.

*It doesn't matter*, Oscar replied. *We have to see it through to the end, or where do you think we'll end up? We prove how committed we are, we prove what we stand for, and the rest… I tell you, the rest will come together.*

It had, clearly. But they hadn't all stayed in agreement about whether that was worth it.

"Winston didn't feel that way," I said. "He thought you'd gone far enough, or he would have come back."

The icy darkness inside Oscar flashed in and out of view again. I caught a glimmer of the same impression in the eyes of the boy next to him. Mildred's lips tightened.

"Winston was an ungrateful wimp and a traitor," Oscar snapped. "He had everything, and he threw it away for who knows what. He threw *us* away."

"Oscar," Mildred said in a weak voice.

Ignoring her, he made a sudden lunge toward me. "If you're so concerned about the gate, why don't you spend a little more time over there? We'll help you find your way."

The edge of his spirit's light crackled against my skin like an electric shock. I winced and jerked away. With a harsh laugh, a couple of the other figures pushed toward me as well. They lashed out with glowing limbs, smacking me as I backed away with increasing speed.

One of the girls whipped around me, a searing heat slashing across my back in her wake, and I stumbled. As I caught my balance on the ground and shoved myself upright, I glanced behind me. My stomach flipped over.

They were herding me toward the gate, yes—and toward a more faintly glowing figure still standing there.

Sylvie watched me with her darkly rimmed eyes, patiently waiting for me to come to her.

No. I wasn't ready—I didn't even know what I could say to her, how I could make any of it up to her. My pulse hiccupped, and I threw myself between two of the school's spirits before they could close the gap that had opened up between them.

"How long does she think she's going to run?" one of the girls said derisively as I dashed for the school building.

"You *can't* keep running, not forever," Oscar called. "There's nowhere to hide."

The throbbing in my wounded calf had spread all the way to my thigh by the time I reached the door. I couldn't run much farther in a totally literal sense. I bolted inside, slammed the door shut behind me, and limped down the hall as quickly as I could manage.

It occurred to me to check to supposed infirmary first, but my quick search of the small room turned up no first aid equipment whatsoever. What more could I expect from this place? I ended up in the kitchen after all.

The press of the towel I tied tight around the wound offset a little of the pain, but it did nothing for the chaos of emotion churning inside me. Maybe I shouldn't have confronted the former staff at all. As far as I could tell, I'd only riled them up more by making them remember past offenses. If they did figure out just how tied to Winston I was, they might not give me another chance to run.

How the hell could I help anyone else get out of this mess when I couldn't even defend myself all that well?

A sense of hopelessness trickled through me as I

hurried up the grand staircase. At least the school's spirits hadn't chased after me inside, not yet.

A mass of a dozen or so students filled one side of the second-floor hallway. Some of them were holding... painting canvases? Marked with sharp lines that weren't paint at all. No, those were bits of twigs and thorns, dark and twisted, pierced through the fabric to hold them in place. I had to hold in a shiver as I recognized the remains of the rosebush I'd hacked apart.

"Come on, come on," a guy said, beckoning for me to slip past him into the apparently sheltered area the outer students were guarding. The ones in the inner circle, who had no shields, circulated with restless murmurs.

As I hesitated, Ryo stood up in the midst of the small crowd. His face somehow both brightened and fell at the sight of me.

"Trix!" He waved his hand in a jerky motion. I scrambled through the other students to reach him and stopped dead at the sight of Elias slumped beside one of the classroom doors. The ghostly figure of a young man leaned over him, half sunken into the wall.

Ryo's gaze dropped to my leg. A faint speckling of blood had soaked through the towel. He grasped my arm. "Are you all right? What happened out there? Did you find Cade?"

"Yeah. And his monster wasn't all that happy with me. I'll be okay." I motioned to Elias, the much more urgent concern in front of us. "Your blockade here didn't totally work?"

"We did work out some techniques for getting the

ghost-things to back off," Ryo said hastily. "Unfortunately we didn't manage to cover every side… and the bits of the dead bush don't seem to be enough to detach these things once they've got their hold on someone."

"How long has he been out?" I asked.

"I'm not sure… Not much more than twenty minutes or so."

My fingers curled into my palms. Of course Ryo must expect me to dive in and help Elias find his way out like I had with Jenson. But Jenson had dashed off after I'd done that. Cade had attacked me after I'd entered his vision. Was intervening even the right call?

"I don't know if jumping in is really making things better," I said, my voice dropping so only Ryo could hear me. "I don't know if I've made *anything* better." Not with this, not with destroying the rosebush…

Ryo's golden eyes widened. He squeezed my shoulder. "I'm not going to tell you what to do, Trix. But—if one of those things grabs me, I know *I'd* want you with me, however you can be there. I wish I could do the same for you."

Could I say the same? Did I really want Ryo seeing the darkest pieces of my past brought to vivid life? He might not say that himself if he'd experienced just how real and wrenching those moments were.

But every second I just stood there, I felt even more helpless. Elias had already been weakened. Better to say I'd tried than to just give up.

Setting my jaw, I reached for the apparition that was gripping him.

# CHAPTER SEVEN

*Elias*

When Trix had explained what happened in the ghost-induced visions, I'd assumed they came on like a dream, unsteady and faded around the edges, wispy to the touch. In actuality, the room I found myself in felt as real as the hallway I'd been yanked out of. The linoleum floor was perfectly solid beneath my feet. The whir of the ventilation system carried clearly from a vent near the ceiling. The sharp scent of pine air fresheners covered up most, but not all, of the lingering stale cigarette odor that had hung in the place when I'd first leased it.

Which had been just a couple of weeks ago, based on that smell and the guy standing in front of me in the midst of the few desks set up in the office so far—all of them empty, the employees gone home for the afternoon. I didn't remember what I'd been doing here in the early evening before Bryan had stormed in, but it wasn't hard to guess. Filing extra paperwork, going over the figures for the day, charting out new plans… Getting a new business off the ground required a hell of a lot of work, especially when you were spending a significant portion of your day at college finishing your degree.

I hadn't seen Bryan face to face—only here and there in the halls, at a distance—since we'd had this conversation in reality. I'd forgotten how worn-down he'd looked then: his normally pressed button-up shirt wrinkled, the collar askew. His pale hair fell across his forehead at erratic angles rather than slicked back straight. My gut twisted.

But this was exactly why I'd done what he hated me for, wasn't it? Because he'd let himself slide; because he'd been spiraling downward faster than I'd felt comfortable predicting outcomes from.

He'd been my best friend since we ended up sitting next to each other in seventh grade, both of us jockeying to earn the top marks and win the most honors, but in a way that'd left us invigorated rather than trying to strike each other down. I hadn't *wanted* him struck down—I'd wanted a real challenge. The times he'd bested me, there'd been nothing shameful about it, because I knew how hard he'd worked for the victory.

And then he'd just… stopped working. Stopped even trying.

When he stepped closer, another smell reached my nose: the tang of alcohol. Bryan swiped his hand across his mouth.

"I can't believe you really did it," he said. "After everything we talked about, everything I put *into* it... This was my idea as much as it was yours, Eli."

What were the arguments I'd given him back then? That I'd come up with the initial spark, so he'd really only spun off from my inspiration? That I'd been the one really willing to put in the time and legwork when push came to shove? I couldn't remember the details, six years later. Only the way he'd shouted at me with insults meant to cut and then stomped off. That and telling myself afterward, with nearly solid confidence, that I'd made the right decision and his outburst only proved it.

None of that mattered now. I'd hurt him—wounded him deeply—and if I'd had my head on straight, I'd have seen that at the time. All the same, the need to explain my actions somehow rose up inside me so fast I couldn't hold the words back.

"I just wanted to get the business up and running so badly, Bry," I said. "I didn't *enjoy* leaving you out. But you weren't ready, and it was starting to seem like you might never be ready—"

"My mom died out of the blue six months ago," Bryan cut in. "My dad went off the deep end with grief. How the hell did you expect me to be thinking about financial analyses and employee retention at a time like that?"

I winced. "I should have cut you more slack. I admit that. I was too much in my head, focused on the larger goals. It wasn't your fault. You didn't do anything wrong."

"You didn't want me to hold you back. You figured you'd outgrown me, that I wasn't worth your time or consideration anymore. I saw you do it to so many other people we hung out with, but I thought I was better than all of them. I thought we understood each other."

The way he'd framed it wasn't so far off from my thoughts at the time. I'd taken the ideas we'd worked on together and gone off seeking investors and resources on my own as soon as it'd become clear he wasn't in any state to talk about the plans.

I could have kept him on board—I could have written him into the documentation so there'd have been a place for him if he *was* ready later. But I hadn't. I hadn't wanted to risk that he'd end up dragging the company down.

"I had a lot of messed up ways of thinking." I groped for the right thing to say. "It was how I learned I had to be if I was going to live up to my grandfather's expectations. He was always pushing me forward, wanting more and more from me..."

"Don't blame this on anyone except yourself. *You* decided to screw over your best friend. *You* decided to throw away eight years of working our asses off beside each other."

"I know. I know. I'm just trying to show you it didn't come out of nowhere. It wasn't maliciousness."

Bryan snorted. "Oh, that makes it so much better. You simply couldn't bring yourself to care about anyone other than yourself. I guess that explains everything. Sure, sure, go on your way now that you've given your justifications."

"I'm not—"

A shape flickered into being at the edge of my vision. My gaze twitched to the side.

Trix had appeared by one of the desks at the edge of the room. She caught my eyes immediately, her expression tight with worry. The slight raise of her eyebrows asked a clear question: Did I need her help to get out of this?

Just seeing her brought me back to the real present— to all the things I'd figured out about myself and my life at Roseborne. So maybe I had needed her, if only just to remind me. The rest I should be able to do on my own.

No explanation was good enough to be worth harping on it. That wasn't what Bryan deserved from me. I shot Trix a stiff smile to say I was handling the situation and turned back to my former best friend.

"You're right," I said. "Forget all that. What really matters is that I'm sorry—for how it all went down, for putting my interests ahead of yours, for not being there for *you* when you were going through a hell of a time with your family... You contributed a lot to the foundation of the business. I shouldn't have cut you out. I was being a selfish, judgmental ass."

Bryan frowned. "And is you saying that supposed to make it all better? I hope you're not asking me to forgive you just like that." He snapped his fingers.

I shook my head. Trix was watching us, silent and still. I didn't love that she was witnessing the end of this confrontation, but *she* deserved at least a glimpse of the damage I'd done in my life before Roseborne.

"How could I expect you to forgive me?" I said. "You were a great friend, the closest one I ever had, and I threw that aside the second it got a little inconvenient. I've realized that I threw away far too many things that were more important than I let myself believe while I was chasing the idea of being a success. Which is even more stupid because that idea wasn't totally mine. Part of me was just trying to make someone *else* happy. I know how fucked up that was."

"So, what now?"

I swallowed thickly. "I can't do anything for you from here, Bryan. If I get out of this place, I'll track you down and see if there's some way I can make it up to you. But I can promise you that I'm already challenging my old ways of thinking, the lessons my grandfather hammered into me, in every way I can. I want to change. I don't want to be that guy who had you storming in here, not ever again. And if I can't get past it, well, then I'll die here without hurting anyone else, and that'll be totally fair."

"Elias," Trix said quietly, her voice a little choked. I didn't let myself glance over at her. Holding Bryan's gaze was hard enough. He stared at me as if he wasn't sure how to respond to the words I'd just said. Then he eased back, turned, and walked out the door of the office.

Did that mean I'd succeeded in whatever test this was supposed to be? I couldn't find it in me to feel triumphant about that.

Trix skirted the desk and came up beside me, taking my hand. I clasped her fingers with mine. Before she could say anything, the scene around us rippled away into darkness.

I lurched back into reality, my eyes popping open to stare up at Trix and Ryo braced over me. I'd ended up sitting on the floor in the hallway, leaning against the wall.

Other students stirred around us, some of them still holding the canvas-and-bramble shields Ryo had come up with. A spark of genius, really. I had to give him credit for that. He might act like a slacker, but he had a quick mind under the go-with-the-flow attitude.

Trix let out a shaky breath and leaned in to hug me. I returned the embrace, unable to resist her touch or the warm citrusy smell that clung to her.

"I'm sorry," she murmured. "I was worried—I wanted to be with you in case there was anything I could do—I guess you had it under control."

"You don't need to apologize." I let go of her so I could push off the wall and leverage myself onto my feet. Then I touched her face, looking down at her. "You did help, just by being there. I got a little off track, and you reminded me to get on the right course."

"I'm sure you'd have gotten there anyway," she said.

"Hey." Ryo touched her side, his gaze intent as he studied her face. "You've been doing plenty, Trix, really. No one else can even *try* to help people once they're caught up by the ghosts. When I try to grab those things, it does squat."

Her head drooped. "What I can do hasn't made much difference. They just keep coming. And the staff—what they've turned into now, anyway—they're watching it all thinking it's great that we're going through even more torture."

She leaned into his touch just slightly, but that was enough to set off a flare of jealousy in my chest. A large part of me had been clamoring for this girl to be mine, *just* mine, from the moment we'd first connected. All the unkind thoughts I'd had before flitted through my head—about whether the guy in front of me or Jenson, wherever he'd wandered off to, were even worthy of her attention or affection.

I closed my eyes for a second and shoved all that away. Hadn't I just promised my former best friend that I was doing whatever I could to change? The competitive spirit, the conviction that I was owed more than anyone around me—those were relics of a past I'd sworn I wouldn't repeat.

Something had obviously shaken Trix's confidence. I should focus on that. When I looked her over, my attention stopped on a makeshift bandage wrapped around her calf. My stomach lurched.

"You're hurt."

Trix looked down at the wound as if she'd forgotten it. "It was… Things got a little tense with Cade. And his beast form has sharp claws." She gave me a slanted smile. "One more thing I need to hash out with him when this is over."

If we could get through it in the first place. Why wouldn't she be struggling when even the guy she'd leaned on most of her life was lashing out at her? When her connection to the school and its history put her in the very center of this conflict, where none of us could support her as much as we'd have wanted to?

We could do better than lashing out like her foster brother had, at the very least. We could offer the *opposite* of what he'd dealt out. Maybe it wasn't a ticket out of here, but if we steadied her convictions, it'd be worth it to demonstrate how much she meant to us, how eager we were to be with her, united.

How much we were willing to set our selfishness aside to give her a momentary escape into adoration.

I craned my neck. A couple more ghosts were gliding along the edges of our little crowd, but I didn't recognize either of them. My jacket still lay on the floor by the bannister, the brambles we hadn't made use of heaped there.

I glanced at Ryo and Trix. "Are either of those ghouls here for one of you?"

They peered at the figures, Trix bobbing up on her toes. "Nope," she said as Ryo shook his head.

I tapped the other guy's shoulder. "Grab my jacket with the rest of our broken rosebush?"

Ryo cocked his head at me. "What are you planning now?"

My body balked for a second before I said the words, but I propelled them out anyway. "I think while we have a bit of a breather from these intrusions from the past, we should collaborate by giving Trix a reminder of just how much we're here for her, in every possible way."

# CHAPTER EIGHT

*Trix*

Elias slid his arm around my back as he guided me toward his math classroom. I shot him a questioning look, and he only gave me a small, secretive smile. Carrying Elias's suit jacket, Ryo met us as the other guy opened the door. The eager light in Ryo's eyes suggested he had a better idea where this was going than I did.

Inside, Elias locked the door—to prevent intrusions from the students gathered in the hall, presumably, since we knew the ghosts would walk right through walls. He took the few remaining handfuls of crumbled bramble from the jacket and dropped the shards along the front of the room and the wall that bordered the neighboring one. A sharp, slightly burnt scent wafted off them and quickly faded.

Elias tossed the last few bits and wiped his hands

together. "I don't think we can count on keeping the spirits out completely, but between that and the others with shields outside, it should buy us some time."

I glanced around the room. "Time for what?" When my gaze settled on the teacher's desk at the front of the room, a trickle of heat ran through me to pool between my legs. Just this afternoon, even if it felt like days ago now, I'd pulled Elias to me there and indulged in a very satisfying quickie.

As if he'd read my mind, the math teacher touched me again, letting his fingers trail down my spine from shoulders to ass. A fresh tingle sprang up in their wake.

"All the chaos has shaken you up," he said. "Made you doubt yourself. But *we* believe in you. I thought you could use a very vivid demonstration of that." His gaze slid to Ryo, who'd come up beside me, and then back to my face. "I'm not going to lie. My first instinct is to try to make you mine and only mine. But if you can handle more than that, why shouldn't you have all the attention you can get? You're worth it."

He met my eyes intently as he spoke, his own turned an even darker shade of brown than usual. I had the sense this offering wasn't just about me. He was making a point to himself too—that he could share? That he could have what he wanted without needing to push anyone else out of the way? That vision of the past had shaken him too.

Ryo dipped his head to press a soft kiss to my shoulder from behind. "I can approve of that initiative—if you want this, Trix. Maybe it'll help you face whatever else is going to come at us tonight."

The heat I'd felt before was expanding all through my body now. In this moment, between two of the guys who'd been here for me and accepted me beyond anything I'd dared to hope for, all the worries and awfulness of the last few hours retreated. Those factors might not be gone completely, but damn did it feel good to let go of them even in part. To simply *think* about letting some other sensation take me over for a little while.

Was it selfish of me to even consider this indulgence when Roseborne was going to hell, perhaps literally, all around us? Probably. But nothing I'd done since chopping down that rosebush had gotten us closer to escaping, and being with these guys, opening myself up to their affections and giving them my trust, had strengthened the power I held inside me before. What seemed selfish might end up helping everyone.

At the very least, it looked like Elias and Ryo could use this temporary escape as much as I could.

I reached up, curling my fingers into the smooth fabric of Elias's dress shirt where the collar opened to reveal a hint of his well-muscled chest. That was all the answer he needed. He bowed his head and captured my mouth.

This time wasn't like before, when we'd practically crashed together in a rush of desire. He kissed me deeply, passionately, but not urgently, as if he wanted to savor the experience as long as he could. At the same time, Ryo teased his hands up and down my sides over my shirt. He kissed my shoulder again, then the back of my neck.

The last time I'd gotten it on with two of the guys at once, Ryo had stayed in a supporting role, coaxing so much pleasure from my body while taking little for himself. He'd revealed to me that the punishment the school had dealt him prevented him from receiving much enjoyment from *anything*, but he'd made it clear that his positive emotions weren't completely dead. I wanted him to get as much as he could out of this encounter too.

When Elias released my mouth, I turned my head and tucked one arm behind me to run my fingers into Ryo's silky hair. He eased to the side so he could catch my lips. His kiss was even sweeter and more tender than Elias's, giving without asking anything in return.

We could all realize that completely chucking off our clothes in our present circumstances wasn't the wisest idea. Elias simply eased my shirt up to reveal my bra. As I kissed Ryo, the other guy stroked his thumbs over the peaks of my breasts, gently and then with firmer pressure, until my nipples strained against the thin fabric. Pulses of pleasure ran through my chest with each caress. My hips started to sway between the two guys, a deeper need kindling between my thighs.

Ryo kissed me with even more enthusiasm, his tongue delving between my lips to twine with mine. His deft fingers glided over my bared stomach and back, conjuring fresh heat in their wake. Elias reached between us briefly to unhook my bra, and Ryo's hands dipped even lower to run over my hips. I pressed back into him automatically, with an electric jolt of anticipation at the unmistakable hardness of his erection against my hip.

Elias dropped his head to kiss my naked breasts. As he charted a careful but determined path toward their peaks, the flick of his tongue sent sharper quivers of bliss over my skin. At the same time, Ryo eased up my skirt. He cupped my sex through my leggings with an unexpected firmness. I gasped, grinding into him, and his breath came out in a stutter. Yeah, he could definitely feel *something*, even if it wasn't everything I'd have wanted to give him.

He rippled his fingers against me, massaging my clit with building waves of pleasure, and Elias sucked my nipple into his mouth. The combined sensations washed through me. My knees wobbled; my fingers clutched at Ryo's hair, at Elias's collar. I found just enough wherewithal to slide my hand down Ryo's body to fumble with the zipper of his cargo pants.

A soft groan escaped him when I brushed his cock through the layers of fabric. He released my sex for just long enough to hook his thumbs into the waist of my leggings and yank them halfway down my thighs, dragging my panties with them. At my wriggle and his tug, they dropped farther, past my knees. I eased my hand inside his boxers and stroked his rigid cock, skin to skin.

Oh, God, yes, I wanted that inside me. If we never made it out of this place after all, at least we'd go with happy memories.

Elias had turned his attentions to my other breast, swiveling his tongue across that nipple while his fingers kept teasing the other. He tested his teeth against the sensitive skin, and I couldn't hold back a whimper. As I shifted my legs farther apart, he trailed his hand down. Just as Ryo aligned himself with my slit from behind, Elias pressed down on my clit. I moaned and bucked backward, and Ryo plunged into me as if he'd been built to meld with me.

I grasped Elias harder to steady myself as I rocked with the other guy's thrusts. Elias glanced up from where he'd crouched before me. Whatever he was searching for in my face, he must have found it. He sank lower, all the way to his knees, and then bowed his head even more. With my next sway toward him, his mouth replaced his massaging fingers over my clit.

The shock of pleasure of his lips suckling me on the outside and Ryo's cock filling me from the inside sent me soaring. A demanding growl I hadn't known I'd had in me reverberated up my throat. I wanted, and wanted, so fucking much, and somehow the colliding waves of bliss were too much to bear and not enough all at once.

Ryo drove into me at an even better angle, and I shattered between them, clenching and gasping. Elias smiled against my sex. He kissed my hip and my belly, easing his way up, until I regained my wherewithal enough to push him back toward the ground. I intended to pay some of that pleasure back.

We all sank down to the floor together, Elias sitting, me and Ryo on our knees. Even with the aftershock of my orgasm still quivering through me, the caress of Ryo's hand over my thigh and then slipping around to finger my clit set off new sparks of longing. He plunged into me again, and I rocked into his thrusts. They sped up, flooding me with a delicious burn.

I kept just enough awareness of my intent to grasp the fly of Elias's slacks. His cock pressed stiffly against it. He let out a strangled groan as I freed him, his arms braced to keep him upright as his head lolled back. I dipped down to take him into my mouth.

"Fuck," he muttered, so raw and unlike his normal straight-laced self that I practically came again just hearing it. His musky flavor filled my mouth. I let Ryo's rhythm guide the bobbing of my mouth, my tongue slicking around Elias's cock, all of us moving together in a mass of rising bliss.

Elias reached to tangle his fingers in my hair, not controlling my movements, only following them. The friction against my scalp made me hum as I sucked him deeper. He swore again, his hips bucking up.

"Trix, I can't— I'm going to—"

Good. The haze of ecstasy was seeping through me too. My awareness seemed to spiral up into the air on that rush, my lips closed more tightly around Elias, and he came with a salty flood in my mouth.

His groan set off a chain reaction. I clenched around Ryo with my second release, a shudder running through me, and he groaned in turn. His thrusts turned erratic. Then he tensed above me and sagged as he found his own peak.

In the afterglow, we managed to gather ourselves enough to sit up, leaning against the back of the desk with me nestled between two of my lovers. For the first time in all the make-outs and hook-ups since I'd arrived at the school, the ones I remembered clearly and the ones I'd only retained glimpses of, not even the smallest pang of guilt hit me.

I was happy. They were happy. We'd made a moment that was kind of beautiful together, even if plenty of people would have thought there was something weird or deviant about it. I didn't give a shit about them. All that mattered was the warmth of these two bodies next to mine —two guys I cared about and who cared about me more than I'd believed was possible just a day ago.

No surge of power had formed in my chest. I guessed our intimacy hadn't provoked much in the way of the sort of energy I needed to tackle the school's former staff and its other terrors. But I did at least feel grounded, calmer, ready to take on everything else we were facing.

Which was a good thing, because as we pulled ourselves to our feet, tugging our clothes back into their proper places, the bits of bramble Elias had laid down along the front wall twitched. A gap opened up between two of the larger pieces, and then the ghostly figure of a slim, middle-aged woman seeped through the wall, making use of that gap.

Beside me, Ryo stiffened. He took a step back and then held there as if he wasn't sure whether to run or brace himself to meet his fate. His breath spilled ragged from his mouth before he managed to speak.

"It's my mom."

# CHAPTER NINE

*Trix*

Seeing the anguish on Ryo's face, I couldn't think of anything except finding a way to free him from it. As the translucent apparition of his mother approached him, I dashed to the front of the room and grabbed as many of the broken brambles as I could scoop up in one motion.

"Maybe we can get it to back off—get you out into the crowd where we have more defenses—"

Ryo was shaking his head. His jaw had clenched, the tendons in his neck flexing. "It's okay. You've all had to make your amends, right? I'm the last person who should be exempt."

He didn't give me a chance to argue or to try to intervene. Instead of waiting for the ghost to cross the last short distant between them, he stepped forward, toward it.

The filmy woman raised her arms and caught him in the eerie embrace I'd witnessed too many times already.

Ryo's head slumped, his eyelids falling shut. He swayed backward to lean against the desk behind him. Then he was deathly still, locked in the apparition's hold.

A lump rose in my throat. My fingers tightened around the brambles, barely registering the prickle of pain their sharp edges provoked.

Elias touched my arm. "I think he'll be okay. Out of everyone at Roseborne, I've always gotten the impression he recognizes his past mistakes pretty clearly."

"Yeah," I said, thinking of the ways Ryo had talked to me before, his acknowledgment that he'd screwed up, hurt people, that he couldn't see himself as better than me no matter what *I'd* done. So much shame had roughened his voice when he'd owned up to his drug addiction and the awful places it had led him.

But I knew how badly I'd fucked up too, I'd never have tried to justify it, and I still wasn't sure I could handle a confrontation with Sylvie. Jenson and Elias had both struggled in the visions I'd found them in, and I wasn't sure those figures had meant as much to them as Ryo's mother had to him. He'd been thrown right into the deep end of this sadistic test. It was harder to say the right words, to snap out of old habits, when you were right smack in the middle of your horrible history in full vividness.

"If you think he might need the help, you can go after him," Elias pointed out. "I'll watch out for both of you."

I glanced up at him, taking in both the professional authority of the young man I'd first gotten to know as my teacher and the passionate vulnerability I could now identify underneath. My mind slipped back to the affection that had shone so clearly in his eyes when he'd made his proposition not long ago and when he'd talked about everything he believed I deserved.

"Another of those things could come for you."

He shrugged. "Then I'll do my best to make my own way out, and if I can't, I'll hang in there until you can come save me too."

His voice turned wry with those last words. I thought about my hesitation to follow him into his own vision of the past. The uncertainties that had gripped me then felt much more distant after the way the three of us had just collided in unity and desire, but I had to ask anyway, "It didn't bother you that I intruded on that moment with your friend?"

Elias's mouth twisted, but in a way that looked more pained than annoyed. "I'd like to be able to take care of my own problems. But I'm not sorry you saw some of that argument. I spent... too much of my life letting myself decide I knew better than everyone around me, that my opinions and desires trumped everyone else's. If you're with me, I want to know it's because *you* decided to be here knowing the full picture, not because I've hidden parts of myself that would have changed your mind."

Hearing him express that sentiment made me choke up even more. This was why Roseborne was so sick, why the staff were so wrong. Elias had changed enormously from the guy he must have been in the scene I'd stumbled into. He could be generous and loving, and he *wanted* to be.

Maybe the college's tortures had helped him get to that place, but they didn't leave him any room to be that changed person in a meaningful way. There was so much he—and Jenson, and Ryo—could have done to actually make up for the harm they'd caused if they could have gone back into their regular lives with their new perspective. Why was it better to just keep torturing them until they were drained of any life at all?

That didn't help anyone, other than maybe giving the spirits who ran this place a malicious satisfaction.

"And that's why I do want to be with you," I said to Elias.

The light that lit in his eyes was even fonder than before. His hand rose to my cheek. He turned me toward him just enough to lean in to kiss me, softly but intently enough that the gesture sent a quiver of pleasure through me.

After, he tipped his head toward Ryo. "You want to be with him too. We're all in this together. I'll be right here waiting."

I stepped toward Ryo's hunched form, a momentary hesitation coming over me. But I didn't even have to ask whether I should go ahead, did I? Ryo had told me to my face that he'd want me lending a hand if he ended up in this situation and I could join him. He might be wondering what was taking me so long—or worrying about what might have delayed me instead of focusing on his own challenge.

Drawing in a deep breath, I touched the ghost that gripped him. My hands slid into its cool aura like the ones before, and I gave myself over to the falling sensation that would transport me into his vision.

The room I landed in hit me with an unexpected brightness. Warm sunlight gleamed through broad windows in a living room that was all pale wood and tasteful linen fabrics. A thrum I thought might have been a dishwasher running carried through the wall.

Ryo stood at one end of the room, a few steps from where I'd arrived. He was facing not just his mother but a similarly aged man who must have been his father and a teenage boy who looked like a younger version of Ryo—his brother, presumably. They formed a cluster by the arched doorway to the dining room, his mother's hands braced on his brother's shoulders as if she thought she might need to defend him.

"Your *grandmother*," she was saying in a tone of horrified disbelief. "It's bad enough when you take things from here. This can't go on any longer, Ryo. Please, you have to let us help you."

How had the Ryo of the past responded to that plea? Denials, anger, pretended remorse that was really just biding time? From my birth parents to a couple of the people I'd hung out with in high school, I'd gotten plenty of experience with the addict playbook.

Now he simply gazed back at them with a slumped posture like the one he'd fallen into back in the math classroom, regret tightening his features, shame radiating from every angle of his body. His obvious remorse brought an ache into my chest. I wanted to reach for him, but I had to give him a chance to say whatever he felt he needed to. I couldn't pass these tests for anyone else, only offer what support I could when needed.

"I wish I had," he said to his family. "I can't tell you how much I do. You have no idea how much I'd give to be able to really see you again and apologize properly. Every day, I remember the crap I put you through and think of all the things I should have done differently."

"It's easy to say that," his brother said, raising his chin defiantly. "Somehow you didn't figure that all out when you were actually here. You didn't care about us at all, just getting high and messing around with your friends. What makes you think I'd ever *want* to talk to you again, no matter what you say?"

Ryo deflated even more. "That's totally fair. I'd never force you to talk to me. I *know* I can't force you to forgive me, if I even deserve that in the first place."

"You ripped apart this family, lied to us, stole from us, threw everything we offered you back in our faces." His father crossed his arms, frowning down at him. "How could you ever have thought that was acceptable?"

"I wasn't thinking at all," Ryo said. "I just—I wanted to add something different to my life, and I picked the wrong thing. Something really stupid. And then once I got started, and my friends were into it too, and it hit me in a way I liked so much… I didn't know how to stop."

"We did everything we could to help you," his mother

said, her tone getting sharper. "We'd have paid for all the counselors and programs and whatever else you needed to get clean, but we couldn't make you go. You didn't even try to fix the mess you'd made."

"I know." Ryo's voice became very small as he hung his head. "I've got no excuses. I was a shitty excuse for a son and a brother—for a human being—and I can't take that back now. All I can say is how sorry I am and that if I got the chance, I'd give everything I have to make it up to you."

I could hear the honesty ringing through his ragged words. Why wasn't it enough for the vision to release him? He was taking all the blame, accepting their judgment of him—what the hell else did Roseborne want from him?

There must have been something, because his father started laying into him again. "How can you possibly believe there's any way to make up for what you put us through? The second you had a chance, you'd probably go straight back to the drugs."

At Ryo's wince, the frustration that'd been churning inside me flared into anger. Before I could think better of it, I marched up beside him and glared at the conjured images of his family.

"What the fuck is wrong with all of you? He obviously feels horrible about how he acted back then. He's telling you that in every possible way. How is beating him up for it over and over helping fix anything?"

Their gazes turned to me for the first time, as if they hadn't registered my presence until I'd spoken. "Who have you brought into our home with you?" Ryo's mother said with a faint grimace. "Is this one of *those* friends?"

"Trix," Ryo said like a protest. Like he believed he couldn't have expected anything better than the hostility they were throwing at him. So, what, he should end up stuck in a loop of his supposed family berating him and him apologizing over and over, for the rest of eternity? Hell, no.

I ignored his mother's comment. "Maybe you need to just leave," I said to him. "I don't know how you could show how sorry you are beyond what you've already said. *I* can see it. Roseborne's pushing for something else."

Ryo glanced toward the house's front hall, his stance tensing. "I can't just leave with them still thinking I don't care."

"They know you care. They've decided it's not good enough."

I paused, taking in his fraught expression, the guilt still holding him rigid. The people in front of him weren't really here other than as projections of his past—of how he pictured them. How he imagined they'd react. It could be the staff or the dark powers that lurked within them and the school had decided he was falling short no matter what he did… or it could be that *he'd* decided that.

I knew that feeling. It echoed through me, taking me back to the moment when I'd confessed to him and the other guys about my messed-up relationship with Cade and how that had led me to the most horrible act of my life. I'd been so sure they'd walk away from me if they knew the whole truth.

But they hadn't. Ryo was the one who'd come to me first. Come to me, held me, and told me he didn't just accept me, he *loved* me, as I was.

A swell of emotion overwhelmed my anger and the pain of seeing him so downtrodden. I could give him the same thing he'd given me, couldn't I? I hadn't let myself even think the words before, hadn't thought I could trust anyone other than Cade enough to really let them into my heart, but Ryo had proven me wrong. He'd brought a joy into my time at Roseborne from my very first cycle on campus. He might have made a mess of his life before, but he made things of beauty now.

I stepped around him to stand between him and his family and took both of his hands. Ryo blinked at me, his expression puzzled. I squeezed his fingers and forced the words past the lump still lodged in my throat.

"I know what it's like to feel you can never make up for the ways you've screwed up, for how horribly you've treated people. All you can see are the bad parts of who you've been. But I've seen who you are *now*, I know who you are, and I—I love you. If you can forgive me, you've got to believe people can forgive you too."

Ryo's eyes widened. Then a glorious smile stretched across his face, beaming so brilliantly it could compete with the sunlight streaming through the windows. It occurred to me then that Jenson had been able to talk truthfully inside his vision. The curses didn't follow the students into the realm the apparitions conjured. Which meant Ryo could feel full happiness now for the first time in three years.

He tugged me to him and kissed me hard, and that was all the answer to my declaration that I needed. I kissed him back, absorbing the sensation of being loved by this man for the first time when he could completely feel that emotion, completely enjoy this display of affection.

Then a sudden surge of energy yanked me away from him and tossed me into a whirl of darkness.

# CHAPTER TEN

*Jenson*

A low wind whipped up across campus, tugging at my clothes and howling through the trees. Night had fallen completely, but the sky was still clotted with clouds. The only light was the pale streams drifting from the school's lit windows, the faint glow on the mist still drifting by the stone wall, and hazy spots here and there where the ghosts that had emerged from that mist now bent over their prey.

With every passing minute I spent out here, searching for some kind of safe haven felt like more of a lost cause. The ghostly apparitions roamed everywhere. Now and then I caught a flash of light at the corner of my vision that told me the staff in their new supernatural forms were still flitting around campus. No doors or walls could hold any of them back.

The only place I wanted to be was beyond that gate,

and I wasn't sure anymore how safe it'd be even out there. Not that the answer to that question mattered, since I wasn't going to find out anyway.

I meandered through the darkness across the overgrown lawn, giving the fallen students a wide berth just in case their ghosts decided to branch out and take on other targets. The wind licked cold past my jacket collar. I was coming around the north side of the school when I nearly tripped over the sprawled arm of a figure I hadn't noticed among the shadows.

It was a guy—face down, nothing distinctive about him that identified him to me at a glance beyond his gender. No glowing form hunched over him. He was just… lying there, as if he'd been tackled and then abandoned.

Was he even alive? Or had his rose split apart into browning petals as limp on the ground as he now was?

A trickle of nausea collected in my stomach. I backed away, hesitated, and then hurried around him. If he was dead, there was nothing I could do. If he *wasn't* dead, I still couldn't do anything. We lived and died by the school's whims and maybe our own actions, no one else's. Otherwise Trix would have saved us all twice over with the strength of her will alone.

I couldn't go back to her empty-handed. The longer I spent out here, the more pathetic it would look if this mission turned out to have been in vain.

I glanced toward the scattering of nearby trees. An urge tugged at me to stop this pointless rambling altogether, to find some place to hide out on my own—

maybe the gazebo over there, not that it'd offer any real shelter—and weather this disaster as well as I could without worrying about anyone else. There might not be anywhere safe on all of campus, but at least then I wouldn't have to feel guilty about not protecting anyone other than myself.

The impulse passed through me, and I shoved it away with a jab of a different sort of guilt. I'd promised Trix I'd come back. I'd *meant* to try to do something useful for her and, well, Ryo and Elias too, I supposed, even if they were much lower on my list of priorities.

I'd told myself I was going to be different. I wanted to be someone different. Or at least, a different version of me. The guy I'd felt like in the moments when Trix had seen past my lies and banter, in the moment when she'd opened herself up to us and I'd come to her alongside the other guys to show her I'd stand with her no matter what she'd done in the past.

It was just hard to hold on to that feeling while I wandered in the dark on my own.

By the time I made it the rest of the way around the school building, the last few students had given up on the gate. I headed down there to test the bars myself, just in case.

The latch didn't budge at my heave. The wrought-iron structure simply let out a dull creak. I peered down the road on the other side, wondering if the view was even accurate. Roseborne was stuck in this constant damp mid-spring weather, but the rest of the world wouldn't be. For all we knew, in reality the trees out there were bright with autumn colors or laden with snow.

The right thing to do was go back, admit I'd come up with nothing, and see if the others had some new strategy I could help with. And keep the hell away from our new ghost friends so Trix didn't have to jump in and watch me at my worst again. If she'd even be all that happy to see me after my recent performance, that was.

I propelled my heavy feet toward the school's front doors. Halfway up the path, my legs stalled.

One of those ghosts was gliding across the lawn toward me. I knew that face, didn't I? My shoulders went rigid.

Yes. Yes, I did. Both from my regular memories and Roseborne's conjured images in the counseling room of the people I'd wronged. His case hadn't been the worst, but it'd been a harsh one.

I could have run for the school building and bought myself a little time. But as I watched him approach, a sense of deeper resolve came over me.

I'd probably have to face him eventually one way or another before Roseborne let go of me. If I took what was coming to me here on the lawn, there'd be no need for Trix to get involved at all.

If I was going to make something of myself other than the manipulative prick I'd spent most of my life being, I had to find my way there on my own, not just when she was looking over my shoulder.

I stayed where I was. The ghostly guy drifted faster. As he reached me, I closed my eyes and braced myself.

A tingling rippled through my chest when he shoved his hands into me. Then I was falling away into a thicker darkness—and out again into a narrow, stuffy office that smelled like old sneakers in a different high school, one that wasn't mine.

The guy I'd just seen as a ghost was in front of me now in full color, laughing and spinning in the chair at the one large desk in the office. My eyes caught on the metal box at one corner of that desk. The club he was president of operated out of this room. They kept their treasury in here. And a couple of weeks ago, this dude—I couldn't even remember his name, for fuck's sake. Matt? Mike? Something generic like that—had mentioned in my hearing that they'd fundraised over a thousand dollars for some initiative they planned to put in motion next month.

Easy pickings. That was all I'd seen. Ever since I'd gotten old enough to pass as a teenager, I'd trolled the high schools around the city, watching for opportunities, for marks. Just like Mom and Dad used to take me around playgrounds and elementary schoolyards when I'd been little, before Dad had been locked up. Although back then I'd been more like bait or a side part placing the seeds of the larger con. These days I ran the whole show.

Matt-Mike had been simple to read. He was overly eager for acknowledgment, wanting to think he was accomplishing great things but afraid he was actually a putz. Which he was. But I'd chatted him up and acted impressed by his stories, and he hadn't questioned why he'd never seen me around the large school before. I fit in well enough. He'd invited me over to his house to play video games. Helped me pull a prank I'd suggested. And once I'd warmed him up sufficiently between the other cons I was running here and there, I'd set him up for the real fall.

In reality, I'd left the room with all the cash in that box within the hour. Matt-Mike had never seen me again. I'd set up enough crumbs of evidence that no one had believed him when he'd protested that someone else had stolen the funds. He'd been accused, convicted as much as any high school administration could, and expelled.

According to the counseling room's playbacks, the expulsion on his record had stopped him from getting into the dream university he'd babbled to me about a gazillion times. He'd always looked kind of broken whenever the white walls had shown me his image.

Because of me. I'd broken him. I could see it now as he stopped the chair and grinned at me—all he'd wanted was a friend. Maybe he'd have been a good one if I'd given him a chance. I'd simply never considered it. Never looked at him as a human being with needs as legitimate as mine, just like I hadn't with Penny.

"I know it doesn't look like much," Matt-Mike was saying now. "But the stuff we've got in the works—I bet they'll write us up in the newspaper. Might even get on TV. You'd better believe everyone'll be signing up for the club next semester."

"I can't wait to see it," I said automatically. "It sounds awesome."

No, that wasn't what I was here for. Roseborne wanted something out of me, wanted me to give this guy something… He'd never had a chance to curse me out. I wasn't sure he'd even been certain I was the one who'd screwed him over, even though he should have been able to guess. Was the school waiting to see if I'd go through the motions all over again? How stupid did it think I was?

What *would* have made this situation better for the guy? If I'd just walked away, I guessed. Of course, then he'd have felt like shit in a different way, because his new best friend had ghosted him for no apparent reason.

I wet my lips. I could be honest in here. After all the time I'd spent lying to dorks like this, it could be that the truth really would set me free. And hell, after a year of being unable to speak it, in some ways even painful honesty should be a welcome change of pace.

The fact that every part of me balked at the idea of confessing only made that theory more likely. There was nothing Roseborne liked more than putting us through the wringer from every possible angle.

While I'd been thinking, Matt-Mike had started rambling about some meeting the club had organized yesterday. I cleared my throat at the first lull. *Just get it over with.*

"Hey," I said, with a prickle of frustration that I hadn't even managed to keep his name in my memory. "Look. I —You shouldn't be telling me all this stuff. You shouldn't have let me in here at all. I'm not really your friend."

He stared at me, his forehead furrowing. "What are you talking about?"

My throat tightened. I waved my hand vaguely. "It's nothing about you personally. I'm not really *anyone's* friend. I'm nice to people when I want something out of them. Which is a shitty way to live, but that's just how I operate. I'm telling you for your own good."

He still looked more bewildered than anything else. "So, you're saying you don't want to hang out anymore? We could do something else if you weren't really into—"

"It's not like that. I just... don't really do friends. At all."

"Why not? What kind of person doesn't 'do' friends ever?"

A reasonable question. I opened my mouth and closed it again. A deeper, sharper truth dug into my chest behind my collarbone. For a second I was afraid if I tried to spit it out, it'd slice me open from neck to chin on the way up.

I swallowed hard. If I could own up to being an asshole, I could own up to this too. Give the fucking school what it wanted.

"I'm a total fraud," I said. "Everything I show you is made up, designed to make you happy to be around me. It's not me. I don't—I'm not even really sure who 'I' am outside of a con. Who the hell would *want* to be friends with a guy like that?"

Matt-Mike shrugged. "You haven't given me a try."

"Why bother?" My fingers curled around the edge of the chair back I was braced against, letting the plastic dig into my skin. "I know you'd never want to be around me if you saw the way I think and the things I've done to people. Why the hell would I want to put myself through confirming that?"

"Sounds like a self-fulfilling prophecy."

"Yeah. One I've fulfilled by being a prick on a regular basis." I looked away. "I'm just saying. Be a little more careful who you trust. It'll save you a lot of hurt. And—I know you don't know about it yet, but I'm sorry for the ways I hurt you. I don't even remember what I did with that twelve hundred dollars. It couldn't have been that amazing."

A pang had spread through my chest, jagged around the edges. It stung my lungs when I inhaled. I closed my eyes against the discomfort, just for a second—and when I opened them, I was sitting on the cold grass of Roseborne's lawn outside the college building.

I stared up at the Victorian mansion in a daze. Getting out of that vision hadn't taken much, had it? But at the same time I felt as if I had dug a knife through my innards to dig that honesty out.

A knife, and… A pinching sensation formed farther back, behind the thump of my heart. Like a petal crinkling, a stem shuddering. A taste like decayed rose flooded my mouth. I had to clamp my teeth together to hold back the urge to vomit.

I'd gotten out, but not in a way that had made Roseborne totally happy. Somewhere out there, my rose was fading.

# CHAPTER ELEVEN

*Trix*

I stumbled out of Ryo's vision of his family, and my back smacked into Elias's chest. He gripped me by the arms from behind—*he* was the one who'd yanked me out. My head spun as I took in Ryo slumped on the desk, the ghostly figure of his mother still holding him in her grasp. Hadn't what I'd said to him been enough?

"I have to go back," I said, shifting forward.

Elias's grip tightened just slightly. "I'm sorry," he said. "I didn't want to interrupt, but—"

He tugged me to the side, and I realized we had extra company. Another translucent figure had passed through the wall: a young man, maybe seventeen or eighteen, with carefully combed blond hair and… one of those maroon school uniforms the spirits who ran this school all wore. The kind I wasn't sure had been worn by anyone since

1927.

Something about the guy's face stirred a quiver of recognition. Had I seen him in the yearbook too?

He couldn't have been looking for any of the three of us. He *shouldn't* have been. Our grandparents hadn't even been born when he'd have worn that uniform. But he was making his way—more slowly and uncertainly than the other apparitions I'd seen, but still with a clear sense of purpose—around the teacher's desk, his gaze fixed on me.

Elias let me go when I went still, but he stayed next to me, his hand a reassuring warmth on my side. "It was obvious as soon as he came in that he was heading for you. I don't know why, or if he'll actually grab you. I just didn't want to find out what would happen if he did while you were still mixed up in Ryo's ghost."

Yeah, that might have been even worse than the visions usually were. We weren't really meant to be able to slip into each other's encounters at all. A collision between two could have been disastrous.

I edged to the side, and the ghost adjusted his course to follow me. There was no denying that it was me he was after. It didn't make any sense. All of the other apparitions we'd tangled with so far had been people from our lives— and not just any people, but people our actions had made a profound impact on. Some kid from nearly a hundred years ago didn't fit the pattern at all.

Maybe he wasn't part of the same pattern. Maybe a different sort of ghosts had been freed by my shattering of the basement rosebush as well. My mouth went dry, but I stopped backing away, propping myself against the side of one of the student desks instead.

"I need to find out why he's coming to me—what he wants," I said. "There's got to be a reason. It might be something that helps us figure out how to escape this place for good."

"Or he could hurt you," Elias pointed out, his stance tensed.

"I think I've got to take that risk. There are a whole lot of other things here we already know will hurt us if we don't deal with them soon." I looked to Ryo, trapped in his own ghostly conflict, and my stomach twisted. "When Ryo wakes up, tell him I'm sorry I couldn't see the whole thing through."

"He'll understand," Elias said. "He—"

Before he could say another word, resolve hardened the features of the ghostly boy. He leapt across the last few feet between us and drove his filmy hands into my abdomen. Elias's voice, the room, and everything else around me whipped away.

With a jolt, I was outside. Outside on the lawn behind the main school building, standing in its shadow at the edge of beaming late-afternoon sunlight. I'd never seen a sky that clear and blue over Roseborne in my present reality. The breeze carried no hint of roses today, only freshly mown grass and the chatter of the students lounging around the pool or sitting in lazy clusters across the lawn.

All of those students wore the same maroon uniform as those in the yearbooks—the one worn by the eight who'd transformed this place into its present horrific state with their bizarre ritual—although many had shed their jackets in the warm air. I'd been sucked back nearly a century into Roseborne's history. Why? How?

I glanced down and realized it wasn't just the people around me who were from the distant past. The body I saw wasn't my own at all. It was clothed in its own maroon uniform, filled out in very different places from my normal figure. No breasts, no hips, and I wasn't going to dwell on the unfamiliar equipment I was abruptly aware of between my legs.

I wasn't Trix in this vision. I wasn't *me*. I was a boy—a slim, kind of gawky boy…

The realization hit me like a splash of cold water. This was Winston Baker, my probable great-grandfather. I'd caught glimpses of memories that seemed to be his before. Apparently enough of him was still in me that his ghosts had come looking for me as well as my own.

Apparently enough of him was in me that it'd worked. Did that mean now I had to work out *his* issues too?

When I raised my head, sucking in a breath to steady myself, I spotted the boy who'd pulled me here chatting with a couple of friends in one of the nearest clusters. He glanced my way with a narrow look as if he thought I might try to join them and was pre-emptively warning me off. Real friendly.

What had Winston done here? What did I need to make up for? How the hell was I supposed to get out of this situation when I only had the vaguest sense of the history?

Several other students joined me in the school's shadow, distracting me from my panic. Not just any students—my seven co-conspirators. Oscar shot me a brilliant smirk that didn't reach his hardened eyes, like a welcome and a threat all at once. Mildred came up next to me with a softer smile and handed me... one of the bows from the Archery room? She was carrying one of her own too—they all were.

I took the bow automatically, grasping it and then slinging the sheath of arrows she also offered over my shoulder. "Ready?" she murmured, and my head nodded of its own accord. The panicked chill crept through my chest again. What the hell was going on? Could I even control what happened to me—to Winston—in this vision?

The other students had noticed us gathering. The blond guy whose ghostly form had approached me stood up with his friends, his lip curling into a sneer. "What are you freaks doing now?"

"They think they're all going to play Robin Hood," a girl near him said with a haughty laugh.

Other emotions bubbled up inside me—ones I couldn't connect to my own mind. Anger and frayed resilience and an urge to strike out; a conflicting queasiness in the pit of my stomach. Winston's emotions from back then.

He'd wanted this and yet he hadn't.

"Almost like Robin Hood," Oscar said, raising his bow with an arrow already strung. "Except rather than stealing from the rich, we're going to cut right to the chase and simply take you down."

In the space of a heartbeat, he pulled back the string and let the arrow fly. The girl didn't stand a chance. The arrow stabbed straight into her chest with enough force to propel her backward a couple of steps. She swayed and crumpled with a gurgled gasp, blood blooming across her white blouse.

Oh, God. The rest of us lifted our bows at the same time as if on cue, Winston included. The boy beside Oscar shot his first arrow straight through the skull of a girl who'd just started to scream. Mildred let hers fly into the gut of a boy who sprang at us as if he thought he could fend off our attack with his bare hands. The others marched forward to take closer shots. My feet, as Winston, moved in time with them even as my mind recoiled.

So, this had been the first blood spilled. *Our blood and theirs*, Oscar had said. Taking their sick revenge for the bullying they'd received. Transforming that violence into the power to torment other bullies and supposed villains across the stretch of a century.

Making Roseborne's new students play out their grand victory tradition in the Archery room, none of us knowing the horrible act we were really repeating. I wanted to puke.

The other students scattered across the lawn with shouts and shrieks. No one else ran at us. Another arrow and another whipped through the air; another body and another slumped on the ground. Winston's arms moved of their own accord, releasing his arrows into the back of a fleeing boy, the neck of a girl who couldn't have been more than sixteen. The fury and the nausea twined together inside me—inside him—in a searing churn.

"Don't let him get away," Oscar called out to the rest of us with a jab of his hand. Then another jab, in a different direction. "She hasn't paid yet."

The others followed his orders as if he were a general leading an invasion. We spread out, stalking across the field, picking off the students before they could reach the shelter of the school. More shrieks, more blood, more sickening thuds of bodies hitting the ground, on and on.

I tried to close my eyes, but Winston wouldn't do more than blink. The effort I put into straining at his arms, trying to hold them back, didn't budge him.

How the hell did I stop him? How did I get me—us—out of this if he was intent on acting out the exact same horror as before?

The lawn was littered with bodies now, red rippling across the bright green grass. One girl had tumbled into the pool. She floated there, face down, blood spiraling around her across the rippling water.

I swung around, my breath hitching, and there was the blond boy from the math classroom. Somehow I'd ended up between him and his route to potential safety. Blood dappled his shirt sleeve from when he must have tried to help one of his fallen friends. As I jerked my next arrow up in his direction, his legs stalled. His hands flew into the air.

"Please," he said, all the arrogance and spite drained from his voice. There was nothing left but raw fear.

"Please." He didn't seem to know what to add to make his case.

Winston hesitated. I didn't know if he had then or if he only was now, with the decades of reflection that had obviously at least partly changed his views on what he and his companions had done on this day. His hand wavered, the queasiness that belonged to him as much as me surging to the base of his throat.

I grasped that chance with everything I had in me. "Don't do it," I said. His lips didn't move, but the words echoed through our shared head. I had to hope he could hear them. "It's bad enough that it happened once. You left this behind. You decided it'd been enough. You can change what you do this time."

"What the hell are you waiting for, Winston?" Oscar hollered from somewhere behind us. "Give that prick what he has coming to him."

Winston's fingers twitched. I swallowed hard and felt his throat bob. "Don't listen to him. He's a power-hungry asshole who roped you in to this massacre to make it easier for himself. You don't own him *anything*."

"It's because of him I'm still here at all," Winston murmured.

"It's because of *you* that *I'm* here at all," I said. "Because you left. Because you picked life and love and making a family over tormenting people. You forgave the people who made you miserable—forgave them enough to let Roseborne go. You can forgive this guy enough to let him go now."

My heart thumped at an erratic rhythm. I wasn't sure

whose emotions were fueling it more. Then, in one sharp motion, Winston yanked down his hands. He dropped the bow and arrow on the grass and exhaled in a rush, his gaze holding the blond boy's.

"I'm sorry. This isn't who I thought I was going to be. I won't go through with it again."

Oscar let out a sputter of anger, and the blond boy took off at a run—and I didn't get to find out whether he'd actually make it to shelter in this rewound sequence of events, because the next moment, the vision chucked me out. Away from the lawn and the sunlight and the bodies speared by arrows, through a rush of darkness and back into the math classroom with its chalky smell and two worried pairs of eyes staring at me.

I clutched at the desk I'd leaned against, catching my balance. The blond boy's ghost had disappeared. So had Ryo's mother. He'd made it through—he was standing in front of me now, a hopeful smile crossing his face as our eyes met. Beside him, Elias was still frowning with concern.

"What happened?" Elias asked. "What did he do to you? It looked like he affected you the same way the other ghosts do."

I nodded slowly, reaching to take Ryo's hand as I did. I wasn't sure if my squeeze of his fingers was more for my reassurance or his. The tangled emotions that had wrenched through me while I'd been inside Winston's past self had fallen away, leaving only my own revulsion at the scene I'd been forced into re-enacting, but I knew what I'd felt. I knew how completely his essence had overwhelmed me. I just didn't know exactly what it meant yet.

"That ghost came for Winston Baker," I said. "I don't know how or why, but I'm pretty sure Winston—part of him is with me. Inside me." My mind tripped back to the moments when that heady energy had risen up inside me before, mine and yet not, bringing memories and unexpected certainty. "I think maybe *he's* the power I've been able to use against the rest of the staff."

As soon as I said the words, the rightness of them reverberated through my chest. Yes. It hadn't just come from him—it was him: his spirit, his will. He wielded just as much power as the other spirits here when I managed to ignite it.

Now if only I could figure out how he and I could shut his former companions down completely.

# CHAPTER TWELVE

*Ryo*

Standing there in the middle of the classroom, Trix looked so determined and yet shaken at the same time that I had to restrain myself from grabbing her in an embrace. I doubted a cuddle was what she wanted while she was trying to work through this revelation, but the sense I had of her own power and the memory of her telling me she loved me brought a swell of emotion into my chest that was difficult to ignore.

We'd already stolen more of a private interlude in this room than I could have expected. We had problems—big problems—that needed tackling now.

"What exactly did you see in the vision if it was Winston's past, not yours?" Elias was asking, brisk and to the point. He wasn't letting himself get distracted by mooning over the strength in this girl, but I couldn't resent him for that. I'd seen the adoration in his expression when the three of us had come together just a short while ago.

Trix bit her lip. I knew before she spoke that it hadn't been anything pleasant.

"I saw what they did to the other students," she said. "The ones they crossed out in the yearbook—and more on top of that, it had to be. They… They must have had an archery club back when Roseborne was a high school, and they brought out the bows and arrows and just shot a whole bunch of the kids who were hanging out on the lawn after classes. They *killed* them. So many people…"

Holy shit. No wonder she looked unsteady. I gave in to my impulse in part, tugging her closer to me so I could slide my arm around her waist. She leaned into me just a little.

"If they weren't afraid to spill their own blood, I guess it's not a surprise they were happy to do it to other people too," I said.

"Yeah. I've gotten the impression the other students were pretty awful to that group. Like, to the point of physically injuring them. But still…" She shuddered.

"And your Winston went along with it?" Elias said. "How did you—or he—get out of the vision?"

"He was pretty angry at the students they were attacking too. And Oscar—the guy who presented himself as the dean to us—was pushing the rest of them hard. But I think Winston was torn about it. He didn't feel *happy* hurting those people. And he hesitated when he could have shot the one guy. I managed to get through to him at least a little, to talk him out of replaying the whole thing. That must have been enough to release us."

I rubbed her back. "It's amazing that you managed to influence him in the moment. If you could convince him to back down, maybe you can sway the others."

Trix ducked her head, the orange strands of her hair falling across her face. "I don't know. He'd already made the decision to leave once, to separate himself from Roseborne. The others have stuck it out. I tried talking to them before, and they didn't care about anything I had to say."

"Well, maybe they do the right thing or maybe we force our way out of here without any help from them." Elias crossed his arms over his chest. Even without his suit jacket and with his shirt lightly rumpled, he made a commanding figure. "We could start searching the staff offices. They could have left behind something that'll give us a clearer idea of how to take them on."

His legs stiffened just for an instant as if he'd held himself back from teetering. The suspicion crept through me that despite the airs he was putting on, he hadn't completely recovered from his collapse. His rose might still be dwindling.

Trix frowned. "I don't know. I think the spirits were pretty careful not to keep anything too personal or important inside the school, except in that basement room. I searched the dean's office and came up empty. Although Professor Hubert—Mildred—did have those pictures with Winston in them." Her gaze turned contemplative. "I think she liked him. Maybe even had a crush on him. It kind of looked like those feelings hadn't completely gone away when I mentioned him to her."

Was that why she'd let Trix make friendly with her in the past week—because she'd sensed the connection? I wasn't sure we'd ever find out for sure. But the thought led me to think of the other person *we* should have been looking out for.

I wasn't sure I could call Jenson a friend, exactly. He'd never seemed to respect me all that much—but then, *I* hadn't respected me all that much for quite a while. He cared about Trix, and Trix cared about him, and just like with Elias, that mattered. I'd found some common ground with our sort-of math teacher. Having another mind in the mix could only help, and Jenson's was definitely sharp if nothing else.

And he'd been gone an awfully long time. I wouldn't wish an extended nighttime wandering around this place on my worst enemy, especially in its current state.

"Before we do anything else, I think we should make sure Jenson is okay and see if he's found out anything useful," I said. "It doesn't seem right for any of us to be off on our own right now."

Elias looked as if he might have argued, but whatever he'd been going to say, he bit it back. Trix's brow knit. "It *has* been a while. I kept an eye out for him when I was coming back from checking on Cade, and I didn't see him."

And Cade hadn't shown up to join us either. I couldn't say I was disappointed about *that*, especially after he'd outright attacked Trix, but the uncertainty of his fate would be weighing on her.

"All right," Elias said. "We go out together, search the campus, and see if we can find him." He shook the few remaining brambles out of his suit jacket and pulled it on, then stuffed a handful from the floor into one of the pockets. "We should bring some of the rosebush pieces in case we run into another of our ghost friends out there at a time when we'd rather not get distracted."

Good point. I didn't regret having faced the vision of my family, as hard as it'd been to finally walk away from them with Trix's words of devotion buoying me along, but that didn't mean there couldn't be bad moments when I'd rather delay encountering whatever and whoever Roseborne threw at me next.

Trix and I bent to gather up the rest of the pieces. I shoved some into the pockets of my cargo pants, and she set hers on the teacher's desk. "Just a second," she said, and hustled out of the room. We followed, stopping just long enough for me to scoop up the bits she'd left, but by the time we made it into the hallway and wove through the crowd still braced there, Trix had already darted up to the dorms and come back down, yanking on her leather jacket.

She accepted the brambles from me and divided them between the two pockets. Then she raised her chin toward the staircase. "Let's go."

We skirted the banister and jogged down the steps. My feet stumbled as we reached the first floor. A girl I recognized from some of my classes, though her name didn't immediately come to me, was slumped limp on the floor off to the side of the foyer. No ghostly form hunched over her. She lay as still as death.

My heart lurched. I hustled over to her. Her body showed no obvious injuries, but when I tentatively swiped the hair from her face, her eyes were open, staring lifelessly at the wall.

Trix came up beside me. Her mouth pressed tight. "There's nothing we can do for her. Roseborne took her just like it did Delta."

And all the other students who'd succumbed to the staff's horrifying powers over the decades. But that answer didn't satisfy me. I'd spent too long being helpless, not even *trying* to get out of this hellhole. I didn't want to walk away doing nothing all over again.

Especially not when the awkward angles of the girl's limbs reminded me too much of a body sprawled broken against asphalt.

I closed my eyes and opened them again, struggling to get a grip on myself. Trix was right. As much as I might long to help, I couldn't here. None of us could bring someone back from the dead. We had to get going to make sure Jenson didn't end up like this girl.

Part of actually contributing was recognizing when you could and when you had to move on. Choosing your battles wisely, my mother would have called it.

The front door's hinges squeaked as we pushed it open. Cold night air flooded over us. I immediately wished I was wearing something thicker than a sweatshirt over my tee.

In the light that spilled from the building behind us, I

made out too many figures sprawled here and there across the lawn. At least most of them were in the grips of faintly glowing ghosts and not completely gone from this world like the girl inside.

We'd only taken a couple of steps away from the building when an undulating howl split the air. Trix's posture stiffened, her head jerking toward the woods.

Cade must be on the prowl. The howl had sounded closer than I usually heard it, as if he were right at the edge of the forest.

I stepped closer to Trix. "At least you know if he's able to do that, he's alive and conscious. The school hasn't really gotten to him yet."

"That's true," she said, but the worry didn't leave her face. After all this time, after everything he'd done to her and the ways she'd realized it'd hurt her, she still felt responsible for saving him.

I loved her for that dedication and at the same time I wished she didn't have it.

We set off in the opposite direction somewhat at random—or maybe Elias led us that way on purpose to avoid any immediate confrontation with Trix's foster brother. Halfway across the lawn to the sparser forest at the north end of campus, a familiar voice careened through the air from behind us.

"Do you think I'm not ready? Give it your best shot, fuckers."

It was Jenson. He sounded pissed off and defiant and… a little crazy, really. If I hadn't known Roseborne wouldn't have offered the means, I'd have thought he was tipsy or high.

We spun around and took off toward the direction his voice had come from, around the back of the school building. Within moments, the streaks of light I now recognized as the staff's supernatural forms came into view just beyond the school. They blazed back and forth in front of Jenson's silhouetted figure, tall and thin as ever, rigid with resolve.

"Jenson!" Trix called out.

He glanced over his shoulder at us and then quickly turned back to the spirits that had confronted him—or that he'd confronted; it was hard to tell. He wasn't holding anything, just standing there empty-handed, daring them to take him on.

Right then, I did like him, at least a little.

As we reached him, the faces of the spirits became clearer—the faces I'd seen in the portraits hanging inside the school every day for the last three years, that I'd tried to replicate during the yearly art contest. Our jailers. Murderers multiple times over.

If they got their way and we all died here even after Trix had destroyed the source of their power, what would they do next? Could they summon up another rosebush in the depths of the basement? Or would they fade away alongside our roses?

From the sharp glints in their eyes and the fierce thrum of their energy cutting through the air, I was going to guess their own fate didn't matter that much to them as long as they took us down with them.

Trix caught Jenson's arm. "What are you doing? You can't fight them."

"Who says I can't?" he said, and pitched his voice toward the spirits. "Do you really think I'm going to just wait for you to throw more crap at me on your own schedule? Come at me and we'll find out who's got more fight."

Whatever had happened to him out here, it'd obviously cracked something open inside him, but I wasn't sure that was a bad thing. Maybe he had a point. The powers that be might still be tormenting, but they'd lost a lot—because of us. Was it really so impossible that we could weaken them at least a little more by taking them on directly?

What was the worst that could happen if we didn't try?

I stepped up by Jenson's other side and elbowed him gently. "Sounds reasonable to me. Even if you've been kind of a prick to me, I'll stand with you."

Jenson blinked at me, looking as if he wasn't sure whether to be gratified or insulted.

Elias joined us with a tight smile. "Sometimes being a prick is useful."

Trix laughed. Jenson rolled his eyes, but I thought his face turned a little brighter at the show of support. I dug a handful of the brambles from my pocket and offered it to him.

"Here, take these. They repel the ghosts a little bit, at least. Not sure about those psychos." I tipped my head toward the spirits.

Jenson let out an amused huff of breath and accepted

the crumpled twigs. Then he turned his gaze on the spirits he'd challenged, shifting it into a glare.

"What do you think? Can you take on all four of us? Too bad you didn't take your chance when it was just me, huh?"

For a few seconds, the blazes of energy simply kept thrumming through the air in front of us. A glimmer of hope that they might back away completely started to form in my chest.

An instant later, they whipped around each other and flung themselves straight at us.

# CHAPTER THIRTEEN

*Trix*

As the barrage of light raced into us, I couldn't stop a yelp from breaking from my lips. The energy of the staff-turned-spirits crackled over my skin with a wavering heat and enough force to rock me backward. I barely managed to keep my balance.

The spirits of the seven former students raced around us and careened through our group again, this time with a smack like an electric current across my face. It stung, but not enough to shift me.

I'd seen them chasing students before—they hadn't actually hurt anyone directly, had they? I wasn't sure they could still inflict the incapacitating headaches and stomach cramps they'd used to punish us during classes. The dispersing of the school's power had changed some things for the worse, but possibly others for the better.

I swiveled on my feet, studying the figures encased by

their bolts of light. Something Ryo had said came back to me—that if I'd been able to influence Winston's thinking in our shared vision, I might be able to sway the other spirits too.

If I could get through to any of them, I knew who it was most likely to be. The girl—woman—whatever—who already had the biggest stake in me and my heritage. My gaze locked on Mildred's streaming dark hair.

I'd grabbed onto the school's newer ghosts. What would happen if I latched onto one of Roseborne College's founders?

No time like the present to find out.

The spirits came at us again, ignoring Jenson's rough chuckle at their attempts to intimidate us, and I sprang at Mildred's wavering form. My hands sank into her light partway into her shoulders. Panic flashed across her face, and suddenly I was tumbling through another stretch of darkness.

The images I fell out into on the other end had a more dream-like quality than the visions the ghosts had provoked. I wasn't in Mildred's head or anyone else's, as far as I could tell. I seemed to be floating by the ceiling of Roseborne's cafeteria, which looked pretty much the same as it did now other than the uniforms the students were wearing.

There was Mildred making her way to the table beneath me, a tray in her hands. One of the other girls from the group of eight walked next to her. They set down their trays with their meals on the table, and a guy in a nearby chair tossed an apple at Mildred's back.

Both girls whipped around, Mildred glowering but silent. With their backs turned, another girl leaned over from the neighboring table, her mouth twisted into a smirk. She dropped something from her palm into both of the girls' mugs, the milky tea absorbing whatever it'd been in an instant.

My stomach knotted. I'd seen where Archery class had originated. Now I was abruptly, sickeningly certain I was about to discover the origins of Tolerance class.

It didn't take long to have my suspicions confirmed. Mildred sat down without saying anything to the guy who'd tossed the apple at her, her shoulders hunched. She took a bite of toast and a gulp of her tea. Less than a minute later, her mouth tightened. A queasy color came across her face. She pressed her hand to her gut like I'd seen students do in Tolerance class after downing the potions we were forced to mix up, but it didn't hold back the effects any more than it would have for us.

She leapt to her feet, wobbled, and vomited all over her breakfast tray and much of the table. A chorus of snickers and snarky comments carried around the room, but before I could focus on them, I jerked away. Some force yanked me from that scene into—

The library. Five heads bowed in a quiet corner between two of the shelves. Mildred was there, and Oscar with his messy black hair. He jabbed his finger toward the other end of the aisle. "We've put up with years of this shit. Are we going to let our whole lives happen like this? People like them are always going to be on top unless we take them down."

"What are you thinking?" one of the other guys asked, his hands clasped in front of him with whitening knuckles. The bruise on his cheekbone suggested he'd suffered at the hands of his classmates pretty recently.

"I say we slaughter them like the pigs they are. I say we've earned that right. I want to see how terrified they look before they get their payback."

Mildred's eyes grew round, but she nodded, a fierce light crossing her face.

The force wrenched me away again, through a blur of darkness and over the grand staircase in the middle of the mansion. Mildred dashed around the second-floor banister to catch up with Winston as he started down the steps. "Hey," she said breathlessly as she joined him, a blush coloring her cheeks. "Are you doing anything after class? I was thinking—"

A guy striding up the stairs shoved purposefully between them at just that moment. He heaved Winston into the banister and kicked the back of Mildred's ankle. With a cry, she tripped and fell, landing on the lower steps and skidding farther down with little gasps of pain.

Her arms had shot up to protect her head. Her elbow jarred and jutted at an unnatural angle as she hit the floor at the base of the staircase. Tears trickled from her eyes.

No one stopped to help her except Winston dashing after her, holding his ribs where the asshole had assaulted him.

Okay, I might not have agreed with mass murder by bow and arrow, but I was starting to see how these kids could have gotten angry enough to resort to those measures. My teeth had gritted on their behalf.

Mildred rolled over on the floor, clutching her probably broken arm, and I hurtled off again, away and down into the dark depths of the school basement.

An undulating, wordless chant echoed off the cement walls. Eight figures stood in a circle in the middle of the room, their faces lit by a little fire they'd kindled in the spot where at some point later Oscar would shove the bloody knife of their sacrifice into the floor and a twisted rosebush would grow. Shadows shifted and twined around them—and a thicker darkness seeped through their clothes, like the wisps I'd seen inside their glow when I'd confronted them earlier.

They didn't seem to notice. Didn't seem to realize they were absorbing something beyond themselves, something toxic. Or maybe that was the whole purpose of this little ritual, whether they'd fully understood the consequences or not.

A pressure gripped me by the shoulders. I had the impression of someone shaking me as if trying to snap me back to reality. And then I did snap out of the basement scene, but not back to the lawn in the night with the spirits blazing around us. No, I was in a hazy, dark gray vagueness with Mildred's face looming just inches from mine. A smell like mildew filled my nose, cool and clammy.

"Winston?" Mildred said, peering at me so intently she might have been looking straight through my skull. Her own head was clearly defined but translucent enough that I could make out the scudding currents of fog behind her. "You came back with her, didn't you? You finally came back."

"He doesn't want to be here," I said. My voice came out hoarse. I cleared my throat and barreled onward. "He left because he didn't believe in what you were doing anymore—in what you'd done before. If anything, he's been helping me try to stop you."

"No." She shook her head, the locks of her hair flying around her face wildly. "He wouldn't—there must have been something— The people out there forced him to stay."

A laugh sputtered out of me. "With the power you all have, do you really think anyone could have done that? He stayed because he wanted to. As far as I can tell, he stayed and fell in love and raised a family. He's *my* family. That's why he's with me now."

I was sure of it then, feeling an energy inside me resonate with the words. Winston couldn't speak, but he made his presence known all the same. And part of him recoiled at the desperation on Mildred's face.

"You don't know anything," she snapped at me. "You're just like them."

I grasped her hand where it clutched my shoulder and held her gaze. "No, I'm not. I think you know that. I've been through all kinds of crap. But I still know that what you're doing here is sick, no matter what anyone you drag into Roseborne has done before. You've made yourselves just as bad as the people you hated. Is that what *you* really want?"

That distant glaze came over her eyes again, her attention slipping away from me and seeming to focus on some point behind me eyes. "Winston, you can't let her talk for you. I need to see *you*. It's been such a long time. Can't you say something for yourself, show me something...?"

"Hey." I squeezed her hand. "Maybe his essence came along with me, but I'm still *me*. And I know him better than you ever did. I've been inside his head, seen his memories—I've felt what he felt during your little meetings. What he went through in the moment when the bunch of you murdered all those kids."

"Kids," she scoffed. "They knew what they were doing, and they got what they deserved. If anything, we let them off easy."

"Winston didn't feel that way. Shooting those arrows made him queasy even while he was doing it. He was angry too, sure—he let that emotion override the rest— but he didn't enjoy it. And if you did, I don't think he'd have any interest in talking to you now."

An angry flush darkened Mildred's face. "He was mine first. He was one of us. You have no idea about any of it."

I fixed her with my firmest stare. The sense of power I'd found inside me before surged through me again. She needed to hear me—she needed to *listen*.

"He was never yours," I said. "Any of yours. You don't get to claim someone. You did know him, at least partly; you saw how he acted, you talked with him, and you watched him leave. Do you really think whatever's left of him is happy seeing you acting like this—talking to his great-granddaughter like this? Maybe... maybe if you could let go of the rage and the need to hurt people and focus on how much you cared about him instead, there is some way you could reconnect with him."

Mildred paused. She searched my face, but not as if she was ignoring me this time. More like she thought I might *be* Winston in some way. The energy inside me stirred, with a tickle of emotion in my chest that reminded me of standing on the edge of the lawn in his memory, accepting the bow and arrows from that past version of her.

He was here with us in his own way. *He* was listening. I had no idea what he actually made of all this or of her, but a flicker of warmth traveled through my chest, like a touch of reassurance. He wasn't pissed off about the things I'd said on his behalf, as far as I could tell.

Mildred's lips parted. Whether she was going to argue more or start to back down, I didn't get to find out. An instant later, I was wrenched backward, away from her.

My mind flashed into blackness, and then I was falling on my ass on the campus lawn. The other spirits streaked by through the darkness. Oscar came at me, his eyes scorchingly bright.

"I've had enough of your idiocy," he barked. "We've got more important things to do than coddle you. You want to see what happens when you try to challenge us? It didn't go well for anyone before you."

He reared back, several other glowing forms joining him in one blazing mass. I scrambled to my feet, finding my three guys still around me. My hands groped out and caught Elias's at one side, Ryo's at the other. Jenson stood next to us, his eyes shooting daggers at our attackers.

"Whatever they throw at us, we can handle it," Elias said.

Ryo laughed, a little raggedly. "They've got lots of big talk, but not much real action yet."

Jenson's lips formed a grin that bared his teeth. "If I'm going to die here, who says I can't make things as difficult as possible for them along the way?"

The words had just left his mouth when the merged spirits charged at us with a roar of energy so loud my ears rang with it. I clutched the guys' hands, not hard enough. The joined lights blasted into our midst and then burst apart with a heave that knocked the air from my lungs and sent me flying away from the others.

I had just enough wherewithal to shield my head. The air whipped past me, my head spun, and I crashed to the ground at the base of a tree. My spine slammed into the roots.

Pain splintered through my back. I groaned. When I willed myself into action, I was half afraid my legs wouldn't move, but they shifted at my attempt to wriggle them.

I had to get up. Oscar and the others might come after me or the guys again.

Wincing at the aches running all through my body, I shoved myself onto my hands and knees and then stood, bracing myself against the tree. More trees surrounded me on all sides. The spirits had thrown me all the way into the woods. Several paces away, I could make out the school's lights between their trunks.

Where had they tossed the guys? I started forward—and my gaze caught on a hunched form, coarse black fur glinting in the muted light, between the trees to my right. My legs froze.

They'd thrown me not just to the woods but straight to my foster brother.

# CHAPTER FOURTEEN

*Trix*

"Cade," I said tentatively, braced to run. A fresh pang of pain echoed through my shin where he'd clawed me. I had no idea how he'd respond to me now in his beast form.

Had he seen me standing with the other guys—holding hands with them? Taking their support the way I couldn't take his? He might be even more worked up than he'd been before.

The furred shape didn't move. In the dim light, I couldn't tell what part of him I was even seeing—his shoulder? His haunch? Was he *okay*?

The jolt of fear that came with that question propelled me forward. I eased between the trees, my nerves jumping at every rustle my feet set off in the quiet of the woods. I'd only taken a few steps when it became clear that the light catching on Cade's beastly fur wasn't just the little that seeped this far from the school.

He was crouched, still and stiff, on the other side of the tree, his wolfish head bowed to the ground. Another of those eerily glowing figures bent over him, hands deep in his back.

It wasn't just any figure. The ghost that had come for him this time... looked like me.

Not exactly the same as I was now. My—her?—hair gleamed with the purple shade I'd dyed it a few months before Cade had left for Roseborne rather than its current brilliant orange. I'd had to throw away the zigzag-pattern top she was wearing this past winter after Mrs. Monroe had "accidentally" spilled half a glass of red wine on me. Seeing the apparition was like looking into a mirror and being faced with a reflection cast from a year ago. A shiver ran over my skin.

How could I be haunting him when I was already right here in the flesh? What unresolved business was this version of me challenging him with? While I'd come to realize that Cade had controlled me and my emotions in ways that didn't sit right with me, that so many times I'd acted more because he'd made me afraid that I'd lose him than because I'd honestly wanted to take those risks or go that far... that was on me as much as it was on him. He hadn't *forced* my hand.

How could anything that had happened between us compare to the people he'd physically hurt in his bursts of temper? It wasn't as if I had anywhere near as much to accuse him of as, say, Richie had.

I guessed I was going to find out the answer to those questions. My heart thumped faster, painful against my ribs, but I already knew there was no way I could just leave Cade to take on this test alone. Maybe I hadn't owed him everything he'd ever asked for, but I'd sworn to stand by him, to save him from this place if I could. Memories of the times he'd swooped in to shield me from harsh words or violent hands flitted through my mind. How many times had he saved me? More than I could count.

I walked up to the joined forms, fighting my hesitation. Would entering this vision go differently because the vision was somehow provoked by a version of me? Could I exist in the same space as my apparition?

No way to know other than by diving in.

I braced myself and grabbed hold of the ghost that wore my face.

The tumbling sensation felt just as stomach-lurching and disorienting as usual. I fell through the now-familiar darkness and landed in a room even more familiar—so much so that I instinctively hugged myself.

It was the little, musty-smelling bedroom Cade and I had shared in the Monroes' house for the past six years. The bunkbed with its lumpy mattresses stood against one wall, the dresser with its wobbly drawers by the one opposite. The desk in between, beneath the tiny window, was barely large enough for us both to set down a textbook at the same time. The rattle of the basement vents sounded just outside—someone was running the clothes dryer.

My foster brother was in his human form, standing to the side of the bunkbed with one hand set against the frame. His body tipped slightly toward the younger, purple-haired version of me in front of him, whose shoulders were braced against the top bunk.

I recognized Cade's pose before I heard a single word come out of his mouth. It was his persuasive stance: close enough to make the moment feel intimate but not so close it was smothering, gaze intent, all attention fixed on his target.

Being the focus of that intentness used to give me a weird mix of emotions: a sort of comfort that he cared that much about my responses, a thrill that there was something I could give him that he wanted, and an underlying jittering of my nerves that this time he might ask for more than I could bring myself to go along with. I'd always ignored the last part as well as I could. Now, when I watched as an outsider, seeing how stiff the other me's posture had become, my uneasiness overwhelmed everything else.

Had I actually looked like that during those moments way back when, tense and uncertain, or was that just Roseborne ramping up the awfulness of the situation? If I had... how had Cade not noticed my discomfort? Wouldn't seeing it have made him back off? He'd always talked as if he only wanted what I was willing to give. He'd just... made it hard for me to feel I could say no without damaging our bond and proving myself less committed than he was.

"Come on, Baby Bea," he said now, in his cajoling tone. That and the nickname raised my hackles in a way they never had before. I didn't think he'd noticed the arrival of my real self at the other end of the room. He brushed his fingers over the conjured me's upper arm. "You know I never meant any of it like that. I have moods. You can't take them too seriously. I've always been here when you really needed me."

The other me raised her chin. "And you held that over my head every way you could. When did I ever challenge you or go against what you wanted? You knew you had me wrapped around your finger—that if you questioned whether I cared enough or went cold, I'd give in rather than risk losing you."

"So it's wrong that I wanted you with me in every possible way? Isn't that what we're all about?" He trailed his fingers lower to the spot where I'd carved up my arm to create a scar that would match the starburst birthmark just beneath his wrist. "Didn't we swear to always be there for each other?"

"It's not really being there for each other if you're the one always calling the shots, and I have to go along with them or get iced out."

"I can't help it if I'm going to feel hurt when you decide you don't want anything to do with me."

"That's it right there," the other me burst out. "It's always all or nothing. You put it out there like I have to either give you everything you want, or I'm shunning you. You *know* that's not true. I can care about you more than anyone else in the world and still have limits."

My throat constricted with every word she spoke. Had the supernatural energies that infected Roseborne seen all those thoughts and feelings inside me, without my even being conscious of them? Were they coming from *Cade's* impressions, what he thought I'd say to him if I ever told him off?

A note of irritation crept into Cade's voice. "Well, sorry if I need to know you're all in. You of all people should know what it's like to be ditched over and over by people who're supposed to be looking out for you. How can I feel good about putting everything on the line for you if I can't trust you'll do the same for me?"

"How can you act like talking me into crazy stunts or into having sex with you is the only way you'll trust me?" my other self demanded. "How are *you* looking out for me if you're constantly pushing me in directions I don't really want to go in?"

"If I thought anything we did would hurt you, I'd never ask you. I've always taken care of you even when you weren't sure, haven't I?"

The constricting sensation in my chest ran down to my gut, clutching my stomach so sharply I winced. He *had* known. He'd basically admitted it. He'd known he'd kept working at me when I wasn't sure, that he was pushing past my resistance… and he'd kept going because he'd decided he knew better what I'd be okay with than I did.

My mouth wouldn't stay shut. "Cade," I said with a rasp.

He flinched and jerked around. He'd clearly been so intent on the vision of me that my appearance in the room had totally escaped him. At the sight of the real me, his back went rigid. His mouth slanted into a crooked line far more sour than his usual wry grin. The other me watched in silent shock.

"Two of you," Cade said in an amused tone that sounded forced. He glanced back and forth between me and my younger self. "Great. Maybe you can talk some sense into this made-up version the college threw at me. I'm taking a real pummeling here, and nothing I'm saying is getting through."

Did he not suspect how long I'd been watching—or was he so caught up in his justifications that he couldn't see how bad the entire conversation made him look?

I took a step toward him. "That's because nothing you're saying makes the things she's pointing out better. You're making excuses, not owning up to it. That's what Roseborne wants—for you to admit where you've done things wrong."

Cade made a dismissive gesture. "This place just wants to torture us any way it can. Obviously this is all bullshit. I know things have been a little tense between us here, but it's *here* that's the problem. All the rest of this garbage—" His gaze dropped to my leg with the makeshift bandage wrapped around it, and his hands clenched. "Shit. Was that me? I remember—it's all kind of foggy when I'm in that state, transformed into that thing—I was so pissed off about my dad and having all those memories brought back up—"

I couldn't let the remorse in his voice deflect me. He was trying to change the subject.

"I'm not upset at you about that," I said quietly. The twisting inside me had turned into an ache so deep the burn of tears was forming behind my eyes. "But the things she's saying aren't bullshit. If you knew I wasn't really okay with some of the things you asked me to do, why did you keep pushing for them? My whole life, all I've wanted was to make *you* happy. It seems like that's all you wanted too. Which doesn't leave anyone taking my feelings into account, does it?"

I saw Cade waver on his feet. He didn't normally show any uncertainty, but between his extended isolation at Roseborne and the emotional whiplash of these visions, even his control must have been getting shaky. For a second, I thought he was going to break down and make a pleading apology. Then his expression hardened.

"I can't believe they've gotten to you too. Warped your mind into thinking I'm just as much of a monster as the thing they forced me to turn into. I guess all that loyalty wasn't worth much as soon as some other guys gave you the time of day, was it?"

The words hit me with a punch of guilt, but anger flared up under it in a way it wouldn't have before, when I hadn't seen what he was doing so clearly. A crack split down the middle of all the memories that had been holding my faith in him steady. How could they mean anything when he was talking to me like this?

Had they *ever* meant anything?

I swallowed past the choking sensation in my throat. "You can't shame me into doing things your way anymore, Cade. I'm allowed to have my own opinions. I'm allowed to say no to you. Just like you've always been allowed to with me. I'm not asking to get away with caring about you less than you do me. I'm asking you to step up and care about *me* as much as I have for you."

"Don't you think I have? For fuck's sake, Trix. It's *because* you matter to me that I want you as close to me as I can have you. You can't expect me to lean back and let whatever happens— I can't just *assume* what you do and say now is enough—" His hands flexed at his sides as he appeared to grapple with his thoughts. His voice turned raw. "People say things they don't mean all the time. People who are supposed to be there for you treat you like shit. You should know that better than anyone, after how your parents were with you. There's no way to be sure."

Was that where this all came from—the rages, the wheedling, the need to jerk me around? The vision I'd seen of him confronting his father echoed through my mind. Did he think that if he had me under his finger, he could be sure he wouldn't lose me?

"Maybe there isn't," I said. "But pushing me around, pushing me into things—that's more likely to make me want to back away from you than anything else."

"Is it? It seems like you were already getting soft on those other guys and leaving me behind before any of this came up. As soon as I wasn't right there to remind you what we have—"

"I'm still here!" I interrupted. "I've been thinking about you the whole time. I never abandoned you. *You're* the one who stayed away from me after I got to Roseborne."

Cade flinched. Then his expression iced over. So did his tone, as he raised a careless shoulder. "If that's the way you're going to see it…" Then he turned his back on me, fixing his attention on my younger self again without another word.

Every instinct that'd been drilled into me over our years together screamed at me to make this better, to show him I wasn't turning my back on *him*—as if that made any sense. As if his rejection were my fault.

I gathered all the strength of will I had in me. The Cade I loved, the Cade who'd protected me—he had existed. The eight-year-old who'd come to me promising we'd get through our time at that first foster home together hadn't been an act. However things had gotten twisted over the years, the genuine devotion we'd started with was still in there. I'd seen hints of it even now during our argument.

I didn't know how his affection had gotten so entwined with this side of him that couldn't believe I'd stay unless he had me on a leash, when that shift had happened, or whether the two aspects could be pried apart. Now that I'd seen it, I wasn't going to give in and beg forgiveness… but I wasn't giving up on him either. That *was* what Roseborne would want, and they were the real villains here.

I turned my own attention on the other me instead of him. "Hey," I said, walking up to her. "You've said enough. It's my turn to deal with him."

"You can't let him get away with the way he's treated us," she said with a cringe.

"It's not our place to punish him. Is that really what you want? It's not what I want. If he won't listen, then we walk away. That's the only way we can really look after ourselves. What Cade decides to do… that's got to be up to him. We have to give him that freedom just like we'd want it for ourselves."

"I'm still here," Cade snapped, but just this once, I ignored him.

"I can't go," the other me insisted. "Not until he shows that he sees. And if he doesn't, I can't let him go at all. No one leaves Roseborne."

That was the school talking much more than it was me. On an impulse, I dug into my jacket pocket. The brambles I'd stuffed in there bit into my fingers. I grasped a handful and shoved it toward the other—false—me.

"I broke Roseborne. I say you let him go—*now*."

Her body jerked as the shattered bits pressed against her collarbone. Seeing my face distort in horror made me shudder, but I held steady. "We're done here. Back off and let this end."

She stumbled away from me, and the vision of the room crumbled away alongside the disintegrating of the shattered twigs in my hand. With a jolt, I found myself standing in the woods again, nothing but dry powder slipping from my fingers—but the ghostly version of me was gone.

The monster that was Cade twitched and hauled himself to his clawed paws. His silvery gray eyes stared up at me. I couldn't read the emotion in them or that fanged face, but I knew what I had to say anyway.

"I'm still going to save you from this place if I can," I said. "You're my brother, and no way in hell am I forgetting that. But—after that's over, once we're out of here, I'm not sure where we'll stand. You need to give me time to figure that out, and you—you've got some figuring out to do too. The one thing I know is we can't keep going the way we were."

The creature let out a low growl through its teeth. A chill trickled through me, but I kept my head high. "I'll leave you to it, then."

A couple of the tears slipped free to slick cold over my cheeks in the night air. The burn of them inside traveled right down the center of me. It took all the strength I had in me, but this time I did turn my back on him, heading toward the school building and the three guys who really had looked out for me since I'd arrived here, wherever Roseborne's spirits had thrown them.

# CHAPTER FIFTEEN

*Elias*

The blast of energy that exploded between me and Trix and the other guys slammed into my chest so hard it lifted me right off my feet. Before I could so much as flinch, it flung me away from all of them. For a few fleeting seconds, the world narrowed down to a blur and the warble of air past my ears. Then I crashed into the side of the carriage house.

A breath sputtered out of me. I pressed my hands to the ground, my fingers digging into the cool earth instinctively—whether to steady myself or to hold on in case another blast came at me, I wasn't totally sure.

My vision was still hazy. I blinked hard, and the shapes of the campus reformed around me in the darkness.

What had happened to Trix and the others? I didn't see them nearby. I moved to heave myself to my feet—and stopped halfway as a wave of dizziness swept through me.

I bowed my head, fighting to regain control over my senses. My legs wobbled beneath me. Just as the strength had leached from my body a couple hours ago when I'd toppled in the basement, weakness seeped through my limbs again. My jaw clenched.

For fuck's sake, I couldn't let myself falter now. I'd survived Roseborne's torments this long. We were so close to breaking free.

I wasn't going to shrivel up like a dead rose when Trix might need my help.

I clenched my jaw and put all my will into straightening my legs. I managed to stand up, but I immediately swayed back against the wall of the carriage house. My breath hitched. For a long while, I didn't dare move, knowing the moment I took my weight off the building, my legs would crumple again.

My grandfather's voice echoed through my head. *Get yourself together, Elias. What kind of a man can't even support himself on his own two feet?*

*You never had to live through anything like this,* I thought back, but I could already imagine his response to that excuse—reminding me of the long journey his family had taken to get to America, of the derision and doubt he'd faced at school, and of how he'd met those challenges and risen above them regardless.

He wouldn't even be wrong. I was failing right now. How could I offer Trix any protection, let alone help free everyone trapped here, when I couldn't even peel myself off this fucking garage?

A fresh twinge ran through my chest. That way of

thinking wasn't helping. I inhaled slowly and fully, focusing on the rise of my lungs and the ebb as they deflated with my exhale. One thing at a time. Elias DeLeon didn't let a bunch of supernatural miscreants dictate his life, even if there wasn't much of it left. If Jenson could take them on wholeheartedly, they'd better believe I could too.

The tremors gradually faded from my calves and thighs. I eased myself away from the building. When my legs held me up, I tried one tentative step and then another.

All right. My head still swam with faint dizziness at the motion, and my heart was beating faster than it should from just that little exertion, but I was getting somewhere now. If I just—

A ghostly form drifted around the side of the carriage house, and all other thoughts fled my mind.

It was my sister. Her face drawn, her dark hair rumpled and pulled back in a wide tortoiseshell clip like it'd been the last time I saw her—the last time I saw her *alive*, that was. She peered at me, her dark eyes plaintive, as she glided closer.

I could hardly run in my current condition. My hand dug into my suit jacket automatically, reaching for the brambles I'd brought with me—but I didn't think I had enough to form a solid barrier around me. She'd find a way through.

Why the hell should I dodge her anyway? Of all the people I'd wronged, Gloriana was the one who deserved my consideration the most. Trix and Ryo had faced the demons of their past in the math classroom without running away. I should have to face this, to relive this moment in all its horrible actuality.

"Gloriana," I said hoarsely. "Of course you'd come."

The ghost didn't speak. As far as I'd seen, none of these figures from our pasts ever did outside of the visions. She just breezed across the last few feet between us and sank her hands into my chest as if reaching straight for my heart.

Cold flooded me, tossing my mind off into darkness. Darkness, and then the clean lines and light leather scent of my last apartment.

Somehow, I was already in the act of holding open the door. My sister slipped past me into the open-concept space with its pale furniture and twinkling pot lights.

It was that day—the last day. The rims of her eyes had turned a harsh red tone; the thick fall of her hair through the clip didn't quite hide the bruise that mottled the back of her neck. She held herself as if on the verge of cowering. As if she saw in me the same violence her "boyfriend" had aimed at her who knew how many times before.

Had I noticed that at the time—how frightened she was of *me*? I didn't remember it. Seeing it now, shame choked me, thick and clammy.

Grandpa DeLeon had always harped about family. Funny how his words about loyalty had only really applied to him and our grandmother. He'd never seen any issue with casting Gloriana aside when she hadn't met his expectations.

And I'd followed his footsteps so willingly.

"I'm so sorry," Gloriana was saying. "I didn't know where else to go. I'm just—I'm so scared, Elias."

I should have hugged her, told her she didn't have to be, that I'd defend her. My arms stayed locked at my sides. In that second, all I could see was how out-of-place she looked in the posh apartment, this teenaged girl with her mussed hair and haphazard clothes. She was everything I'd tried to make sure I'd never become. She'd *chosen* that. Chosen to defy our grandparents, chosen to take the lazy route while I worked my ass off.

No. I closed my eyes, shaking my head at myself. Those were the old ways of thinking that Roseborne was trying to stuff back inside my head. I wouldn't let the college drag me back down that path.

When I opened my eyes again, my sister was backing away. She'd taken the shake of my head as a rejection of her. "Please, Elias," she said. "I know it's a lot to ask. I just need a place to stay for a little while until I'm sure—until I'm sure he won't come after me. I'll help clean up, I'll cook. Whatever I can do to help."

What would she say if I took the same approach I had back then: chided her for her bad decisions, told her she had to live with them now rather than drop them in someone else's lap? Would she have accepted it like the real Gloriana had or laid into me the way Bryan had in his vision?

Better to never find that out.

The words stung coming up my throat, but I forced them out. "I should have let you stay, no cleaning or cooking or anything else required. *I'm* sorry. You needed a brother, and I treated you like… like you were practically a stranger. If I could do this over, I'd tell you to stay as long as you need to. I'd sit you down, and we'd work out a plan for how to deal with that asshole. I—I failed you, Gloriana."

Was I going to do the same with Trix, all over again? Not in the same way, but by giving in to a different weakness also inflicted by someone holding their power over me?

My sister had stopped where she was in the doorway. Her expression showed only startled disbelief. "How can you say that? It's my fault. I ran off with him—I abandoned all of you. I've been so selfish the whole time."

Would the Gloriana I'd known have admitted that, or was this some new test from the college to see how I'd respond? The truth was, I didn't really know. I'd barely spoken to my sister in the close-to-a-year after she'd moved out of our grandparents' apartment to devote all her time to the asshole who'd seduced her—a prick who was almost thirty to her barely legal seventeen. How could any of us have seen that as *her* crime?

I wasn't going to lie to her about what I'd thought back then. Maybe what was true would be enough, as long as I gave her the truth about myself too.

"Maybe you were selfish in some ways," I said. "But you're a teenager. I think you're allowed to make mistakes and be a little selfish. I've been selfish too, and I'm old enough to know better. I was more than old enough to follow my heart and what I believe is right instead of always worrying about what Grandpa would think."

A hint of defiance came into her stance. She crossed her arms over her chest, her lips pursing. "You only just decided that now? It didn't seem like you saw me as anything other than trash back then."

"I know." My head bowed. Emotions tangled through my chest, too tightly wound to pick them apart. Suffocating. What did she need me to say? What could I possibly say that would make up for abandoning her to the abusive jackass who'd killed her just days after I'd turned her away?

"You still think it's true," she said quietly. "You think I'm a screw-up, a mess, that I'll never amount to anything. The only reason you'd help me is out of pity. Of course. I mean, it's obviously true. Only a screw-up would end up begging for help like this. It's not like I'll ever amount to anything more."

"No." My head jerked up. One clear impulse shot through the turmoil inside me. She couldn't believe that about herself—*I* didn't believe it.

She was reaching for the door. I snapped out of the grip the room had held on me and grasped her arm gently to stop her.

"Come here," I said. "Let's just sit and—and talk." While I figured out how to put this anguish into words.

"What's there to talk about?"

Okay, then I'd find a way to say it here. I swallowed hard.

"It doesn't matter how many mistakes you made before. You can always do something different later. I'm trying to do that right now. There are so many screwed-up people out there… but they still deserve to live and get more chances to make something of themselves. Not just the things Grandpa thought mattered either. Things like realizing your relationship isn't safe anymore and getting out. Things like being a brother who's there for his little sister when she needs him."

Like letting her know how much I cared now, regardless of whether it was too late in reality. Like doing whatever I could to help Trix and everyone else at Roseborne even if it wasn't as much as I'd have liked to. Maybe it was true that I'd failed people—hell, I'd probably fail plenty more before my life was over, if I got to live much more of it. I could let that define me, or I could make the most of the parts in between.

"Grandpa expected us to be perfect," I went on. "But *he* never was. He never loved us like the parental figure he was supposed to be—he never figured out how to relate to you. He left me thinking my only worth was how much money I could make and what concrete victories I could show off. *That's* screwed up. So what if we're not perfect either? So what if we fail sometimes? What matters is what you're doing right now. You pick yourself back up and keep going, keep trying."

Gloriana's gaze searched mine. "Do you actually mean that? Or are you just trying to make yourself feel better?"

"I wish I could make *you* feel better. I wish you were really with me to hear this." I raised my hand to brush my fingers over her hair, and then I found I could offer that hug after all. I wrapped my arms around her. She clutched my suit jacket and leaned into me, as if I'd been the brother she'd needed all along.

Something else I hadn't even known I wanted to say wrenched up through me. "I love you. Even if I let myself act as if I didn't, even if all Grandpa's attitudes clouded over it—I've always loved you. I never forgave myself for making you leave that night. Love should have mattered more than anything else."

My sister looked up at me, the tension gone from her face. "Maybe you should forgive yourself now. If we're all allowed to make mistakes. If what matters is how we make up for them."

With those words, she slipped from my grasp. A whirlwind surged around me, tearing us apart, flinging me out of the apartment and back onto the campus lawn outside the carriage house.

I found myself groping into the darkness as if I could have snatched onto my sister and brought her back with me. Of course I couldn't. Unlike some of the people from these visions, she really was gone.

Would she have forgiven me that easily if she could have come back from the dead? I didn't know. But maybe… Maybe what I'd said *was* true for me too. Where did I go from here?

I dragged in the cool air and took a step forward. Another. Another. My muscles were still weakened, but that was okay. I'd make do with what I had.

Out there was another girl—a girl I also loved. That was true too, wasn't it, even if I'd hesitated to admit it to myself before? It was a very different kind of love than I'd felt for my sister, yes, but just as meaningful. And this time I wouldn't let my doubts overwhelm it. This time I'd let it guide me and take as much strength as I could from that.

I had to keep remembering this, no matter how many times those old instincts kicked in: it wouldn't matter how much I ended up being able to offer, only that I offered all I had.

# CHAPTER SIXTEEN

*Trix*

The back of my neck prickled as I emerged from the woods, my ears alert for any sound of Cade following me. I wasn't totally sure whether I'd have wanted him to at this point, despite my original intentions. But what I'd told him was true. I'd get him out of here if I could—and the time for sorting out the rest of our issues would be afterward.

He didn't come after me. And as soon as I'd left the trees behind, my gaze snagged on another slumped figure in an apparition's thrall several feet across the lawn from the woods. I hustled over, peering at the body in the thin light cast by the ghost that gripped it.

It was a girl, her long, fawn-brown hair fanned around her limp head. She looked like she might have been even younger than me, so one of Roseborne's newer students, probably. I recognized her vaguely from around the school, but I'd never spoken to her or shared a dorm bedroom with her, at least not that I recalled. The ghost bending over her was a girl too, around the same age.

My first impulse was to walk away. She wasn't my responsibility. I had to get back to the guys, make sure they were okay. But as I took a step to the side to avoid her body, something twisted in my chest. That way of thinking felt way too familiar.

Like Winston with his group of vengeful students, seeing everything in terms of "us vs. them." He'd attached himself so completely to his small circle that their influence had swallowed up his identity.

Like me and the sway Cade had held over me all these years. I'd been so wrapped up in his narrative of the world that I'd nearly lost real devotion when it was offered to me because I'd found it so hard to believe.

Obviously I wasn't going to be BFFs with every person in the known universe. But maybe... maybe it wasn't such a great approach to focus *only* on the people I cared about the most. I didn't really think anyone deserved Roseborne's treatment, and that included this girl, even if I didn't know her name or anything about her. If she was new, she wouldn't have had much time to process her supposed crimes.

If I didn't help her, there was no one else here who could.

I hesitated for a few seconds longer, and then I moved closer, digging my hands into my pockets. The broken remains of the basement rosebush had helped repel the ghosts on other occasions. I jabbed what felt like my second-last handful at the ghostly girl now, watching her reaction.

The glow around the translucent body flickered faintly, but the apparition didn't move. Her expression didn't change. I pushed harder with no more result.

All right, so once they were attached to their target, that connection must provide enough fuel to make it much harder to dislodge them. At least from outside the vision. I'd been able to get the other me to back off using the brambles from inside Cade's.

Or had that only worked because it was *me*?

I guessed I might find out now. I shoved the remaining bits back into my pockets, braced myself, and grasped hold of the ghost.

I fell with a jerk and a whirl, and stumbled at the edge of a forest clearing. Not the same forest I'd just left, though. The trees that loomed around me stood twice as tall as those on Roseborne's campus. A tangy pine scent wafted through the warm air. The sun beamed down from a clear sky between the canopy of dark green leaves and needles.

The girl I'd seen lying on the campus lawn was bustling around the clearing in a furor. A collapsed tent already sprawled on one patch of ground. She shoved packages of food and cooking utensils into a huge backpack. After she'd swung that over her shoulders, she reached for the tent, started to fold it, and then let out a sound of exasperation and simply bundled the fabric and poles up in a jumble. Then she spun around and spotted me.

"Shit!" she yelped. The tent fell from her arms with a clatter of the poles. She snatched it back up again. "I don't know what the hell you're doing here, but I've got to get—"

If she'd thought she'd somehow be able to avoid the coming confrontation, she was wrong. The ghostly girl who'd leaned over her in the real world, now solid and in full color, stalked into view between the trees from down the slope. She held a towel tight around her body, and her hair was slick from a recent swim. She blinked at the first girl. "What are you doing, Melanie?"

"Getting out of here. I would have been gone already this time if *she* hadn't distracted me." The first girl—Melanie?—jabbed her finger toward me. "There's nothing to talk about. I'm still going."

"But—you're taking all the stuff? I've got to get changed if we're leaving now."

"You're not leaving. Just me. You can figure out your own way home. You shouldn't have—if you hadn't— It wasn't my fault. You deserve this."

"You're going to strand me here with just what I've got in my pack?" The other girl's face flushed. "That's—that's awful, and ridiculous. You're kidding me, right?"

"I told you, there's nothing to talk about. Deal with it."

Melanie turned with a swish of her hair and a huff, but her eyes were wide with a hint of panic. She wasn't actually angry, just trying to flee the conversation she thought was coming. As if Roseborne and the vision it had conjured would let her off that easily.

"Hey," I said, moving to block her way. "You're not getting out of this… this memory like that. Whatever you did wrong, you need to try to make amends for it. And I'm betting you did do something wrong or you wouldn't be here."

Melanie's chin jutted out. "I was totally justified with what I knew. It's not like it's going to hurt her all over again. None of this is *real*."

*It is real inside your head*, I thought. And that was the only place that mattered if she was ever going to get *out* of her head alive.

"That's not the point," I said, keeping my voice as calm as I could. "This is just one more of the college's tests. Do the staff ever let you get away with a half-assed effort?"

Her lips pressed into a flat line, but she stayed were she was, obviously recognizing that I was right.

"What the hell is going on here anyway?" I glanced from her to the other girl and back again. "I'm guessing if you were camping together you must have been friends. Why would you take off on her in the middle of the woods?"

"Melanie is my best friend," the other girl said in a mournful tone. "Or at least she was."

"Shut up." Melanie's shoulders had risen defensively. She grabbed my wrist and tugged me away from the clearing, farther into the woods, where her friend couldn't overhear the conversation. Several paces in, she stopped and turned to me.

"You don't understand. She—while she was down there swimming, I was checking something on her phone, and I saw all these messages between her and my boyfriend. Talking about meeting at a restaurant and what a good time they'd have and shit like that. It was *obvious* she was sneaking around with him behind my back. Who needs enemies when you have 'friends' like that?"

I had the feeling whatever I found out next would reveal that it was her friend who should be asking that question about Melanie. "And then what? Did you do something worse than strand her here? Did something happen to her because of it?" I couldn't see Roseborne targeting her just for flipping out over a romantic betrayal.

Melanie swiped her hand across her mouth. "When it really happened, I called her out on it before I left. She said they'd just been planning a surprise for me—for my birthday. I thought it was a stupid excuse. You have no idea— the whole time we've been friends, she's always one-upped me, acting like she's so much prettier and smarter and better than me. The guys always go for her first. Then one of them wanted me more, and it made sense that would piss her off."

The pieces were starting to click in my head. "But it turned out she was telling the truth, didn't it? There wasn't actually anything going on between them. She hadn't betrayed you at all."

Melanie was silent for a moment. "No," she admitted finally. "I didn't go far enough back in the messages. My boyfriend showed me the entire conversation from his end when I got home. But I had every reason to believe—"

"What happened to her after you left her?" I said, cutting her off. The excuses were starting to grate on my nerves. With the chip in her shoulder that big, I was doubting her interpretation of her friend's previous behavior too. How many other ways had she punished the other girl for acting "better" before it'd come to this?

Melanie glanced away. "We came in my car. So of course I drove that back. And no one else came out this way for a few days. The weather got colder, and she had hardly any food… By the time she found someone who could give her a ride back to civilization, she was sick. Really sick. She spent a week in the hospital recovering from hypothermia and some other stuff."

Ah. "So, you abandoned your best friend in the middle of nowhere, didn't try to get any help for her when you realized she hadn't made it back quickly, and it was all over a huge misunderstanding you didn't trust her enough to let her clear up."

"Well, of course it's going to sound awful when you put it like that."

I wasn't sure there was any way I could put it that *wouldn't* sound awful, but fine. I motioned toward the clearing. "You know now that she didn't actually deserve it. Don't you feel at all bad about what she went through?"

Melanie shifted her weight from one foot to the other. "I try not to think about it. It wasn't *really* my fault. All the evidence made it seem—and I told you what she's always been like…"

Impatience wound through my chest. While I was trying to talk sense into this jerk, who knew what was happening to the guys or, hell, everyone else around Roseborne? I wasn't going to let her off the hook of facing up to her fuck-up by trying to banish the ghost by other means.

"It's up to you," I said firmly. "I've stepped into a lot of these visions now. I know how they work. You need to own up to how you hurt her and honestly apologize, or you're going to be stuck in here for I don't know how long. Maybe forever, or until Roseborne sucks the rest of your life away."

Melanie opened her mouth with another sound of protest, and I raised my hand to stop her. "What's more important to you—avoiding admitting that you went too far or *staying alive*?" Was it really that hard a choice?

Apparently it was, from the way Melanie waffled for another minute or so. She glared at the trees around her as if they were somehow at fault and then glowered at me as if I'd arranged the whole thing. I was on the verge of walking off and leaving her to deal with this problem on her own—there had to be a way I could cast myself out of her vision even if it hadn't ended yet, right?—when she sighed.

"Okay," she said in a small voice. "I guess I should talk to her. I never did after, not exactly."

Thank the Lord. I trailed behind her as she picked her way between the tree roots back to the clearing. Her friend was still standing there, looking bewildered.

"You came back," she said with audible relief.

"Yeah." Melanie set down the tent. She met her friend's eyes and then glanced away. "I do know now that you didn't really do anything with Jake. And… even if you had, you could have died because I left you out here. That was a horrible thing to do any way you look at it. I was just so *mad*…"

Oh, God, don't get back into the excuses. I cleared my throat, and her shoulders twitched.

"Why would you think anything would happen between me and Jake?" the other girl said. "I was so happy you got together with him—you guys make an awesome couple."

"You're just always…" Melanie scowled at her hands and managed to raise her eyes again. "You're so much better with guys. It's hard not to worry. But I still—I shouldn't have been such an asshole about it. I actually felt really horrible when I found out you were in the hospital. I only wanted to freak you out a bit, make it a little hard for you. I wasn't thinking clearly. I'm sorry about that. Sorry I didn't do anything to help you sooner."

Her stance was still tensed, but I believed the shamed note that had come into her voice. It appeared that Roseborne did too. They stood there for another moment, and then the forest scene cracked apart. With a whoosh of momentum, I tumbled back into the school lawn.

Melanie stirred on the grass. She pushed herself up gingerly and looked toward me. Her eyes narrowed and then softened again, as if she wasn't sure whether to be pissed off at me or grateful.

I'd take both. "I'm betting that's not the worst incident in your entire life," I said. "It's only going to get harder— and I might not be around when the next one comes. Remember what I told you, okay?"

Her jaw tightened, but she nodded. I couldn't tell if

she would survive another, more intense vision, but at least I'd given her some tools. I'd helped her through one.

I headed back across the lawn with a minor sense of accomplishment. As I peered through the darkness, my pulse leapt—and then stuttered.

Jenson was standing near the maintenance shed by the side of the school. But he wasn't looking toward me. He was watching a ghostly figure that had slunk around the side of the school and was now heading straight toward him.

*Jenson*

My shoulder was still aching from smacking into the shed when I saw who was coming for me next. I rubbed my arm, watching the ghost approach, and my stomach balled into a knot.

Of course he'd be here. Davin—I remembered *his* name. I probably would have remembered from the time I'd spent working my con around him anyway, but the images the counseling room had shown me of his funeral had solidified it even more.

He glided toward me slowly but steadily. His eyes, always a little watery-looking, stayed fixed on my face. I backed up a couple of steps, debating my best move.

I'd been able to handle the ghosts before. I should be able to face this part of my past too. But my outburst at the assholes who ran Roseborne had left me feeling drained. I wouldn't have minded buying myself a minute or two to be sure I had my head on straight.

I tossed a few of the brambles Ryo had passed to me onto the grass between us. The ghost slowed, considering them. And a voice carried across the lawn.

"Jenson!"

It was Trix. My head jerked around in time to see her jogging over the grass to meet me. Her face looked paler than usual against the starkness of her dyed orange hair and her black leather jacket, but the determination I loved so much in her still shone in her eyes. It bolstered my own resolve and sent a shiver of nerves through me at the same time.

She'd seen some of my past exploits, but nothing like what had gone down with Davin. That situation had been extreme even for me.

It *had* still been me, though. I couldn't brush it off. If I hadn't let myself stoop that low, maybe I wouldn't have been here at Roseborne at all.

If Trix couldn't stand the sight of me after she knew, it'd be my own damn fault.

"Are you okay?" she asked, her breath coming short as she reached me.

I spread my arms as if to show that I was. Easier than trying to form a true answer out of a question or demand. "You?"

"Yeah. Just… been dealing with ghosts I didn't expect." She glanced at Davin's filmy form. He'd taken in the brambles and was easing his way between them with a delicate weaving back and forth. It wasn't going to take him long to reach me. "I take it that's another of yours."

"Isn't it obvious?"

The words rose up to tell her that I'd be fine tackling him on my own—that she should go check on Elias and Ryo and make sure the spirits who'd orchestrated our torture here hadn't visited even more on them. My voice snagged in my throat.

I could do this. Opening up to her was even more important than proving I wasn't the same guy I'd been back then to myself. Maybe it was the largest part of proving that. It wasn't strength to insist on doing everything myself when that was all I'd ever done. The real bravery came in asking for help. In admitting I'd rather have her with me than not.

I held out my hand. "Don't think I can't get through this on my own. And be aware that… it's going to be bad. Will you come with me anyway?"

She studied me. No doubt my awkward reaction after the first vision she'd followed me into hadn't escaped her. "Are you sure?"

I offered her a tight smile. "Why shouldn't you see me at my worst? Isn't it better you find out now rather than later?"

At least then, even if I did die here, if my rose crumbled away because I hadn't fulfilled what Roseborne wanted from me quickly enough, I'd know any affection she still had for me was real. No cons, no hiding behind a practiced persona. Just Jenson Wynter in all his manipulative assholery and whatever else she believed I'd made of myself since then.

Trix nodded. She took my hand just as the ghost made it past the last bramble. Her fingers squeezed mine. I might have tugged her in for one last kiss—knowing it really might be the last kiss I ever got from her—if the conjured version of Davin hadn't leapt across the last few feet to reach me.

Losing my grip on Trix, I fell through the whirl of blackness without any certainty about where I'd find myself on the other side. In the office building where I'd set up a significant part of my scheme? In the bar where I'd first met the guy, first laid the trap, and planted more seeds as it went on? He and I had never actually spoken after it'd all gone down—there'd been no real confrontation.

It was neither of those places, but when my feet thudded onto the concrete surface, I couldn't say I felt any surprise. Frigid wind gusted over me with a fishy scent. Cars roared by at my left. And to my right, just a few steps away from me, Davin stood by the railing of the bridge, in just the right spot so that when he clambered over and flung himself off, he'd hit the highway below rather than the river on one side of it or the shrub-dotted hill on the other.

I'd never been here before, but I'd seen this scene at least a dozen times on the shifting walls of the counseling room. My stomach constricted into an even tighter knot than before.

Davin hadn't hauled himself up onto the wall yet. His hands clenched the railing so tightly his knucklebones stood out against the skin. He looked around, and his gaze caught on me. His body went rigid.

"What the fuck are you doing here?" he said, sounding more hollowed out than angry. "Come to get your last laughs in? I guess it wasn't enough to destroy everything that mattered in my life unless you got to watch the fallout."

I crossed my arms over my chest against the wind. A glance over my shoulder showed me that Trix had followed me as I'd suggested, standing a couple of feet back. Davin didn't pay her any attention, but that was hardly a surprise either. He had too much of a beef with me to worry about anyone else.

"I don't want to watch this," I told him, with the honesty the visions allowed that loosened my chest just a little. "I never meant— This wasn't what I was aiming for. It was just a scam, a way to make some money."

"And to let someone else take the blame. I didn't just lose my job, you know. They sued me for everything I had. I lost the house—the education funds. My wife walked out with the kids a week ago, and she hasn't talked to me since. Did you think about *any* of that? Why the hell did you pick *me* when I hardly had anything to begin with?"

I could recall the answer easily just looking at him. That suit he was wearing, the same one he'd had on in the bar that first day—I couldn't have known he hadn't been able to afford clothes that posh himself, that it'd been the one gift his father had managed to give him before passing on. That he'd worn it even though he was only on the lowest rungs of his company to try to set expectations that he'd be climbing the ladder soon.

That wasn't the whole reason, though. I'd figured out he wasn't a big fish quickly enough during that first conversation. I'd almost walked away. Any other person, any other day, I probably would have. But the self-satisfied smirk he'd shot me and the words he'd said were still burned into my memory, sharp enough to provoke a jab of anger even now.

I'd realized a long time ago that I hadn't gone after him because he was a good mark. It'd been personal, a sick sort of revenge. I'd just never admitted it out loud before. But Trix needed to hear it—and maybe this version of Davin did too.

"I approached you to figure out what I could get out of you because you looked like a big shot," I said. "And then, even though you weren't—there was that news segment on the TV over the bar—you started mouthing off about people who end up in jail. Laughing about how they're doubly losers because they were too lazy to bother making a living without breaking the law and too stupid to avoid getting caught."

Davin waved his hand through the air carelessly. "Why should you care about that? You're still walking free. Obviously your problem isn't stupidity."

My teeth clenched for a second before I managed to unlock my jaw. "My dad's been in jail since I was nine, you prick. You don't know a single thing about him or why he felt he had to look after us the way he did. You don't know how many cons he managed to pull off because he *did* know what the hell he was doing. He never would have taken a risk that could have ripped him away from us if he'd known— That was the *last* thing he wanted—"

I couldn't quite finish the sentence. Funny how back in the real world I couldn't tell the truth, and in here I was struggling to tell what I was afraid might be a lie. Deep down what made me angriest was that I wasn't sure Dad had been lazy or stupid, but I did suspect he'd slipped up where he shouldn't have. That he'd gotten tired of family life, of constantly moving to stay ahead of the law… and he'd given up on himself and on us. On me.

Davin stared at me. "Are you kidding me? I was just shooting my mouth off. How the hell could I know anything about your dad?"

"That's not the point. You shouldn't have—"

This time I cut myself off on purpose. I was getting riled up all over again with the same angry heat that had fueled my schemes before. That wasn't what I'd come here to get sucked into.

I forced myself to inhale slowly. I was pissed off, sure. The guy in front of me was kind of a prick, sure. Neither of those things had justified ruining his life. I could admit that.

The much bigger prick in this scenario was me.

"You're right," I said, each word like a shard of glass dragged up my throat. "Going after you was petty and unfair, and against my usual principles, which I did have a few of. I let my personal feelings mess with good business sense. The point is never supposed to be to totally wreck someone's life. But I didn't let myself think that far ahead. I'm sorry. I should have backed off as soon as I knew you were hardly making ends meet."

"Sorry doesn't do me much good now, does it?" Davin said. "I've still lost everything. Are you going to give it back to me somehow?"

My lungs constricted. How could I? Out in the real world, he was already dead. And even if he hadn't been— "I can't turn back time. I can't reverse what happened. Would it help you to pretend I could? Even if I went to your company and claimed I was responsible, do you think that would fix much of anything for you? They'd still blame you for letting me hook you."

"You could at least offer to try." He held my gaze for one last fleeting second, his eyes wild. Then he swiveled toward the railing and threw himself upward.

I hadn't known I had it in me. I didn't even realize I was going to move until I was already lunging forward. But somehow every part of my body reacted automatically in a way it never had before—toward the danger, rather than away. To help someone else rather than to cover myself.

I flung my arms around Davin's waist before he'd quite gotten his knees onto the railing. He heaved forward, and with a lurch of my gut, I thought we were both going to tumble over. Maybe the fall would have killed me too. All I had to do was let him go in that last moment.

But I didn't. I clung on and hauled backward with all the strength I had in me.

We swayed together. My feet skidded against the

concrete. Trix called out something I couldn't hear over the blood rushing past my ears. Then, my breath stuttering, Davin and I toppled back onto the sidewalk.

My tailbone jarred against the concrete. Davin landed half on me with an elbow to my ribs. I coughed and winced—and kept my fingers dug defiantly into his shirt.

Davin gazed up at the sky. He didn't make a move to repeat his attempted suicide. After a few seconds, he started to laugh, hoarse but genuine.

"You saved my life, you fucking bastard," he said without any hint of rancor.

"I owed you," I said. As the truth of that statement shot through me, the vision ripped apart and hurtled me back to the world where I couldn't speak anything but lies.

# CHAPTER EIGHTEEN

*Trix*

Jenson's vision tossed me free so abruptly that I fell back into the real world with a thump of my shoulder against the side of the shed. Jenson teetered in front of me and caught his balance against the wooden slats. He dragged in a breath and expelled it with a rasp as if he couldn't get quite enough air.

I couldn't imagine what he was going through after the scene he'd just relived. I reached for him and tugged his lean frame to me. His head bowed next to mine, his arms coming up to return the embrace almost hesitantly. A faint tremor rippled through his body.

"That guy really jumped when it actually happened," I said, making what seemed like a reasonable guess. "You didn't manage to stop him."

"Would you believe I wasn't there to even try?" Jenson

said. The rasp had come into his voice too. "What better way could Roseborne guilt me than throwing shit at me I had no idea was even my fault? Be grateful you never had to go through the staff's idea of counseling."

He hadn't known about the suicide until after he'd gotten here? What an awful thing to have hanging over you. "Are you sure it's even true? They didn't make it up to torment you?" All the other visions and the rest seemed to be taken from the students' real lives, but that didn't mean the vengeful spirits never tossed more horror into the mix.

Jenson was silent for a moment, maybe grappling with the right way to get across his answer. "Isn't it plausible that he'd have felt that hopeless after the way I screwed him over? Remember *that* part was true." He made a sound of frustration. "And isn't it kind of them to let me say what I actually mean when I'm off in a fucking nightmare but not anywhere else?"

Despite the harshness of his words, he sounded more defeated than anything else. His arms tightened around me and then started to let go as if he felt he needed to. I held on to him, looking around, and drew him with me toward the door of the shed.

"You should sit down for a minute or two. Get your bearings."

He grimaced, but he didn't argue. He followed me into the small room and sank down next to me on the little cot against one wall. The cot that had revealed Cade's presence on campus to me a few weeks ago. None of the faintly lingering scent I'd caught then reached my nose now. All I breathed in was a hint of dust and a mossy, lightly musky whiff from the guy sitting beside me.

Jenson leaned back against the wall. His throat worked with an audible swallow. He looked at me, his bright blue eyes shadowed in the dim space.

"Don't stay if you don't really want to be around me," he said. "How could I blame you if you don't?"

My own throat closed up at the simple, nonjudgmental question. He really thought I might want to wash my hands of him—because he'd hurt someone in a horrible way? He knew I'd done the same thing. Maybe for different reasons, maybe he'd done it a lot more than I had, but he'd been in Roseborne's grasp paying for those decisions for a year now. And I knew he was a hell of a lot more than a con artist and a liar.

Where could you start laying blame, really, when someone followed the only path they knew how to? Like I had with Cade, like Elias with his grandfather.

I slipped my arm around Jenson again and leaned my head against his shoulder. The heat of his body melted some of the ache that had filled my chest while I'd watched him come clean with his former victim.

"I'm not in any position to judge you," I said. "Not for what you did before. I'm going by who you are now, by how you've treated me, by the ways I can see you've changed. That's what counts. And I want to be with that guy. I *admire* that guy."

Jenson gently gripped my arm to turn me all the way toward him and hugged me even closer. For several beats of our hearts, he just held me, his breath tickling warm over my temple. His fingers stroked over my hair. Then he said, low and soft and with enough emotion ringing through the words that there was no doubting what he actually meant, "I hate you."

I'd never have thought it was possible to say that statement so tenderly. For a second, I choked up too much to speak. I gulped down that lump and tucked my head to the crook of his neck. My reply came easier now that I'd said the words once to Ryo. My whole body resonated with how much I meant it.

"I love you too."

Jenson's chest hitched, and then he was cupping my cheek, tipping my face up so he could kiss me. I teased my fingers over the back of his neck and kissed him back hard, in case he needed more convincing. The longing that radiated from him into me kindled a spark that ran from my chest right down to my core.

One kiss blurred into another and another. We only came up for air in quick gasps before we dove back into each other. Jenson's fingers ran up and down my torso, tracing heat to the surface of my skin like lines of flame, as if he were trying to build layer on layer of pleasure and reassure himself of how real I was at the same time. The need inside me flared hotter.

I leaned back, pulling him with me, until my head hit the pillow. Jenson braced himself over me, drawing out the next kiss until I was practically quivering with desire. I ran my hands up under his shirt, and his breath stuttered with his own longing. He eased up and bowed his head over mine.

"Trix?" he said. The fringe of his hair tickled my forehead. In the darkness, I couldn't make out much more than a glint in his eyes and the vague shapes of his features. But I knew him, now and before—and from other times I might have lost the details of but that still lived inside my mind. I knew his past and how it weighed on him. I knew everything I needed to.

"I want you," I said quietly. "Like you are, right now. There's nothing you need to prove to me or make up to me."

It was absurd how much I wanted him when I'd just been with Ryo and Elias earlier tonight, but at the same time it felt totally natural. We were all tied together in our own weird ways. For all the awfulness Roseborne had thrown at us, it'd also created something like a miracle in bringing us together.

Jenson still hesitated. "Are we safe from those ghosts anywhere on campus? Or from…"

From the spirits of the former staff who could return to harass us, or who knew what else. I found I didn't really care.

"Probably not, but we'll deal with that when it happens. You were right in what you said before—that we might as well make it as hard as possible for the assholes running this place to take us down. And I think we should get in as much happiness as we can too. In case we don't get a chance later."

My heart squeezed at the thought of losing the battle we were fighting—losing my life, him, the other guys, everything. But those words cut through whatever uncertainty had been gripping Jenson. He dipped his head to capture my mouth with his, even more determinedly than before.

I caressed the compact muscles lining his back and then slid my hands up over his chest again. When my fingers brushed over his nipples, an encouraging noise worked from his throat. I tweaked them, and he shoved aside my jacket to return the favor. His thumb swiveled over the peak of my breast firmly enough to send a jolt of pleasure through me despite my shirt and bra.

"Do you have any idea how much I want you?" he murmured, his lips grazing mine with the most torturous friction. "Just let them try to tear us apart."

I hummed in agreement and then let out a gasp when he flicked his thumb with more force. My hips arched up. Jenson grinned at me brilliantly and tugged my shirt higher so he could release my breasts from my bra.

I wriggled and growled between kisses as he worked me over. His skillful fingers stroked every inch of my curves. I yanked his shirt higher too and hugged him to me with a kiss that was all heat and tongues, wanting to feel his bare skin against mine. Imagining what it'd be like to totally strip down with him and enjoy an interlude like this with all the privacy and time we deserved.

Eventually. Maybe even soon. We *had* to get out of this place, if only because I didn't want to waste away without finding out just how good it could be with three guys who truly cared about me, out in the real world without curses or spirits confining us.

But this—this was plenty good all in itself. Jenson

gently rocked against me through our next kiss, his hardness settling between my legs, and set off a deeper pulse of bliss. My desire turned blazing. I pressed up into him, and he groaned.

Urgency seemed to rush through both of us at the same moment. I jerked at the fly of his slacks, and he pushed up my skirt. When he sat up to help me with my leggings, a new urge came over me, one that set off a tingling right down to my sex.

I squirmed out of my leggings and panties, leaving them dangling from one calf to avoid dislodging my makeshift bandage, and nudged Jenson down onto his back. He raised an eyebrow at me as I straddled him, but his eyes gleamed even brighter than before. I kissed his chest, slicking my tongue over one nipple and then the other, and reached between us to grasp his erection.

As I eased my fingers up and down his silky hard length, an inarticulate sound broke from his mouth. He bucked into my hand. I bent to kiss him and lowered my hips at the same time so I could rub his cock against the dampness between my thighs. He kissed me back, rough and ragged, his hand coming up to clutch my waist.

He couldn't have any doubt about how much I was invested in this moment, how much I was getting out of it too.

He and I—and the other guys as well—had been alone for a long time, hadn't we, even if it'd seemed like we had some kind of company? Not anymore. We were making something better of ourselves, something constructed out of love and forgiveness, together.

I lined up Jenson's length with my opening and slid down onto him. He groaned against my mouth. Without a word, he matched the rhythm I set, his hips pumping up as I bobbed down to meet him, plunging deeper and deeper each time.

The delicious burn spread through my hips, tingled down my legs and up to my heart. I rocked faster, chasing the ultimate explosion of bliss. Jenson kept his hold on my waist and brought his other hand to my chest to tweak my nipples. When a needy whimper fell from my lips, he dropped his hand lower, trailing over my stomach. His thumb found an even more perfect spot just above the point where we were joined.

At the first press of my clit, pleasure rushed through me twice as potent as before. I kissed him sloppily, bucked into his thrusts even more urgently. A trembling raced through my muscles. So close. So fucking close—

The wave of ecstasy I'd been riding crashed over me. I cried out, unable to hold back the sound. Jenson tucked his arm around me and managed to flip us over on the cot without slipping out of me. He plunged into me faster, harder—and I shattered all over again as he found his own release with a shaky exhalation.

We eased to a halt, our bodies still locked together. Jenson pressed a delicate kiss to my cheek, my forehead, and then my lips. As our breaths evened out, he gave me a wry but fond smile.

"What's there to regret except the fact that we can't stay like this?"

I smiled back at him. "Nothing I can think of."

We *couldn't* stay like this, though. Guilt was already starting to creep through me when I thought of the short time I'd avoided everything else we were up against on campus. We shifted apart, grabbing our clothes. I'd just tugged my skirt straight over my leggings when the shed door thumped.

I froze. It couldn't be a ghost—one of those could have walked right through the surface. What—

Something scraped against the ground outside, and the door flew open with a bang that snapped the latch. Cade's beast landed on the threshold, his eyes glowering and his fangs gaping to emit a snarl.

## CHAPTER NINETEEN

*Trix*

"Holy shit." Jenson backed up so abruptly his shoulders hit one of the shelving units. The tools and other odds and ends stashed there rattled.

Cade growled again, his coarsely furred form silhouetted by the pale moonlight outside. It glanced off those viciously curved fangs and the silvery eyes set deep in his wolfish head. He stalked a couple of steps into the shed, forcing me to retreat too.

"Cade," I said, holding up my hands and keeping my voice as even as I could. "You can get control of yourself. You're still *in* there—I know you are. Listen to my voice. Remember who I am and who you are. You're not this monster. You can't let Roseborne turn you into one."

I couldn't tell if anything I'd said had sunk in. He'd said everything was foggy when he was transformed like this. The creature swung its head from left to right, studying us. The muscles along its back bunched.

"Hey," Jenson said in the bantering tone I'd often heard him put on with the other students. At this moment, I could hear a thread of tension running through it. "What're you looking so grim for? Why don't we chill out like civilized people and—"

Cade lunged. The space was so small that I'd been standing partly in front of Jenson, but the beastly form knocked me to the side, onto the cot, on its way to him. They fell with a thump and a hiss of pain through Jenson's teeth, his head knocking against the wall.

I shoved myself off the bed and flung myself at Cade without giving myself a chance to hesitate. With those claws and those teeth—it might not be the spirits and their roses that killed Jenson.

"Stop it!" I shouted, digging my fingers into the thick fur. A pungent odor like spruce and spoiling meat filled my nose.

I hauled back, and Jenson thrashed and kicked. The monster slashed its claws across his shoulder and snapped at his face, far too close for comfort. Before Cade could take a real bite out of him, I slammed my elbow onto the beast's jaw.

Cade's head jerked to the side. I smacked his face again, trying to push myself between him and Jenson. Even in the dimness, I could make out the dark patch of blood spreading swiftly across Jenson's shirt. Another was forming lower down at the side of his belly where Cade must have gouged him before.

The creature snapped again, this time at me. The curved teeth rasped against each other with a grating knife-like sound that set the hairs all over my body on end. I shoved the beast by the shoulders, and Jenson landed a kick just beneath its ribs. Cade heaved back and lashed out again. A clawed paw raked across my forearm with an immediate, bone-deep burst of agony.

I choked on a sob and outright punched him, right in the muzzle. "Get the fuck away from us! You fucking asshole!"

My voice shook, but even in his monstrous state, something in it must have penetrated the haze of aggression that had come over my foster brother. He shuddered, balked, and then lurched back a few feet, his gleaming eyes never leaving us for an instant.

Blood dripped from my wounded arm to patter on the floor. Jenson heaved himself partly upright with a wince. "Are you all right?"

"You should be more worried about yourself." I sure as hell was. We both needed to wrap up these wounds and stop the bleeding. But it was hard to think beyond the massive dark shape still looming at the other end of the room between us and the door.

As if to put proof to that worry, a low growl reverberated from the beast's throat. My body tensed automatically. I shifted so I was directly between it and Jenson.

"Don't you dare," I said, fighting to keep my voice steady. "Just get out of here. Get away from us. I know you can manage that much."

The beast didn't budge, though. And in that moment, as I stared him down, it was suddenly hard to see only a deranged creature that Roseborne's spirits had created. Those *were* Cade's eyes glaring back at me from within their frame of fur. The accusation in them, the defiant tilt of the thing's head, the unspoken possibility of violence coiled all through its muscled body…

The staff hadn't conjured any of that out of nothing. Even if the human part of him wasn't totally in control, they'd drawn on what was already there in Cade when they'd created this form, hadn't they? I was looking at a monster, and I was also looking at my foster brother, in a way I'd never let myself see him before.

The pain had radiated all the way up to my shoulder blade. I clenched my jaw against it and glared right back at Cade. The hope I'd been holding onto all this time, even as it frayed more and more, finally snapped. All the hurt and frustration that had been building since I'd first started to recognize his hold on me rushed to the surface and onto my tongue. And then tumbled out.

"You know what?" I said. "I was wrong. You *are* a monster. You go around trying to bully and intimidate everyone into doing what you want, you make them feel like shit if they don't happen to agree, you *batter* them if they piss you off enough. You want to talk about loyalty? How loyal are you if you're going to slice me open the second I show I'm not going to live totally under your thumb anymore, huh?"

Cade's ears flattened back on his head. Another growl seeped from between his fangs, but he stayed rigidly still.

I took a step toward him, my good arm rising, my hand balling into a fist. "You promised to protect me, and you knew I'd do anything to protect you. I came all the way out here and let Roseborne take me for a chance to get you out. I've put everything on the line for you before. And in return for that, you pushed me into all kinds of things I didn't really want to do, you made me constantly afraid that I wouldn't be good enough, strong enough, willing enough for you to want me around. It doesn't matter how much I mattered to you that you wanted so badly to make sure I'd stay—it wasn't *right*. That's not how real love works, Cade. It never was, and it never will be."

"Trix," Jenson said quietly. I couldn't tell if he was trying to warn me, to suggest I'd said enough, or if he was simply acknowledging my pain. Either way, I wasn't backing down. Not until this monster got the hell out of my way.

I stepped even closer with a stomp of my foot against the floor. "Didn't you hear me? Get going! I don't want you anywhere near me, not like this, maybe not ever. I will…" I cast around and snatched a heavy wrench off the shelf beside me. "I swear if you try to take another bite out of me or Jenson, I'll hit back with everything I've got. I don't want to, but I will. So don't fucking try me."

The resolve in that threat must have sunk in. Cade shifted his weight on his paws. Then, with a ragged huff of breath, the monster wheeled and barged out of the shed the way it'd come.

The wrench fell from my fingers to thud on the floor. My shoulders sagged, both with the release of my fears and the rising dizziness I assumed was thanks to the blood still streaming from my wounded arm.

Fuck. I had to deal with that—I had to help Jenson with his wounds—

Jenson had staggered to his feet. I opened my mouth to protest, and my legs wobbled. He caught my good arm, and we both slumped onto the edge of the cot.

"I'm sorry," I said. "I'm sorry. I didn't know he'd— I never thought—"

"Don't for one second think this is your fault," Jenson said, his voice taut but the direction of his gaze making it clear any anger he felt was directed at the creature that had vanished beyond the doorway and not me. "Is it safe for us to go out there with him lurking around?"

"I don't know." I sucked in air and grabbed hold of all of the self-control I could summon. "We should bandage ourselves up as well as we can first. Just to stop the bleeding until we can get to someplace where we can wash the wounds and bind them more carefully." My gaze fell to the surface we were sitting on. The sheet was dingy, but it would be easy enough to cut and fold. Beggars couldn't be choosers.

Ignoring the throbbing in my arm, I pushed back to my feet and found the gardening shears where I'd left them after I'd replanted Violet's rose. How was she handling Roseborne's current state, as weak as she'd been? I hadn't had the chance to check in on her.

I'd get to her when I could. In a few broad snips, I cut off a wide swath of the sheet. Then, with unexpected inspiration, I cut right into the thin mattress. That would do as a makeshift gauze pad.

I set the chunk of foam stuffing against the gouges on Jenson's abdomen and tied them there tightly with the strip of sheet. The only sign that the pressure hurt was the twitch of his jaw. He stopped me before I could bandage his shoulder the same way and pressed the second "pad" I'd cut to my arm insistently.

A different sort of pang, one I didn't mind, filled my chest. "So stoic," I said, as much as I dared to tease after what had just happened.

The corners of Jenson's mouth quirked up a smidgeon. "Real men show no pain," he returned.

The beginnings of a smile faded from his lips as I, with bandaged arm, finally took care of his other wound. When I eased back to examine my work, he studied my face.

"Did he attack me because I was with you?" he asked, in a tone that was barely a question. "Because we…"

"Hooked up?" I filled in. Calling what we'd shared less than half an hour ago a "hook-up" felt much too casual for the emotions that had come with it, but "made love" would have sounded too corny and "had sex" too clinical. There just weren't any good, simple terms to describe what it was like to join your body with a person you cared deeply about that didn't have a mushy, Grandma's Harlequins vibe.

Jenson inclined his head, not quite a nod. I bit my lip as I considered the question.

Who knew what Cade's senses could pick up when he was in that monstrous form? I'd already suspected that he'd ramped up his criticisms of the guys after he'd noticed some kind of intimacy between them and me. And since then, I'd made it clear to my foster brother that I had no intention of or interest in doing what I'd done with Jenson with *him* ever again.

He'd wanted me wrapped around his finger. That much was becoming clearer every time I was around him. He'd wanted to be able to snap those fingers and know I'd jump. Offering someone else a closeness he thought only he deserved—yeah, that could have enraged him. I couldn't say I was sure Jensen and I had been quiet enough that his ears wouldn't have picked up the sounds, especially when I'd left him so close to the edge of the forest.

But all the same—

I tucked my arm around Jenson's. "It doesn't matter. He was pissed off about something. There's *nothing* he could have been pissed off about that would justify that rampage. He doesn't own me. He doesn't get to decide who I spend my time with or what I do with my body. What's important is making sure he doesn't hurt you, me, or anyone else like that again."

A soft little smile returned to Jenson's face. "How can I argue with that?" His features tightened against a wince as he leaned toward me, but his kiss was nothing but sweetness. My nerves had still been jumpy in the wake of the attack; his touch settled them.

When I got up, I grasped his hand to steady him as he followed me. "If Cade's out there waiting, then we defend ourselves as well as we can. He's not dictating how I live my life anymore. We need to find Elias and Ryo—we should *all* be together against… against everything here."

I let go of Jenson to pick up the wrench I'd dropped. I didn't want to come to real blows with Cade again, especially not with a weapon, but I couldn't be stupid about this conflict either. He'd proven I might need to go that far to defend myself.

We slipped out into the night. The clouds had finally drawn back, allowing a thin sheen of moonlight to shimmer across the whole lawn. I scanned the area around us warily, but I didn't see any sign of Cade. Had he slunk all the way back to the forest in his defeat? In his shame? Did he actually recognize that he'd been wrong?

Another question we'd have to deal with later. For now I was just glad that it looked as though we could leave here unassaulted.

As we came around the school building, Elias's broad-shouldered frame had just reached the corner opposite us. He stopped at the sight of us, resting his hand on the bricks, with an expression both relieved and exhausted. From the way he held himself, I suspected the night's events were wearing down his reserves of strength more than he wanted to admit.

"Have you seen Ryo?" I asked him.

He shook his head. "I've been in a vision a lot of the time since we were tossed apart. I'm not sure what direction they threw him in."

"Over the hills and far away." Ryo's familiar mellow voice reached us a moment before he came into view behind Elias. He joined us, walking with a noticeable limp. At the flash of concern that must have shown on my face, he held up his hand to ward off any fussing over his injury. "I landed badly on my ankle. I don't think it's too serious." His gaze paused on Jenson's and my bandages. "What happened to *you* two?"

"It's… a long story," I said. "I was hoping we could find better materials to patch ourselves up inside. At least we've gotten the four of us back together like we set out to do?"

"Even if it was a heck of a trial getting there," Ryo said.

We climbed up the front steps and stepped into the foyer warily. In an instant, Ryo's good cheer drained away.

His eyes had locked on a ghost that was just drifting out of the hallway that led to the staff offices. The translucent young man turned to face him at the same moment, and immediately glided straight toward him. He didn't look any different than the previous ghosts had seemed to me—but from the sickly cast that had come over Ryo's face, he might as well have been faced with the Devil himself.

# CHAPTER TWENTY

*Ryo*

Somewhere in the back of my head, I'd known this moment was coming. How could it not? The guy moving deliberately toward me as a ghost-like image had lost way more because of my selfishness and carelessness than anyone else in my life, even my parents. And not just him, but the others I'd no doubt see as well once he reached me.

My stomach flipped over. A clammy sensation had spread over my skin. I didn't deserve to avoid this, so I wasn't going to try, but—the most intense urge I'd ever felt twisted through me to tell Trix to stay out. To make sure *she* never saw just how much ruin my addiction had caused.

Did I deserve to be spared that either? Hell, no. With the impulse came a rush of shame. I couldn't bring myself to say anything at all to her, too afraid of what might slip out between my competing emotions. Instead, I stepped across the polished floorboards of the school foyer to meet my fate.

The glowing wraith with Kadri's face grasped hold of me from the inside out. The invisible force I'd felt once before flung me away from the grand staircase and the gleaming chandelier overhead, through a churning dark tunnel, and into the driver's seat of my mom's silver Toyota Camry.

My senses jarred at the sudden transition. The world around the car was whipping by with the vibration of the engine pushed twenty miles over the speed limit. A punk rock tune blared from the speakers, almost drowning out the laughter and cheerful shouts of my three friends around me.

The buzz of a recent high sang through my veins. My head felt as if it were full of crinkling cellophane. Salt laced the air from the fast food drive-through meals we'd picked up a half hour ago. Beside me, Kadri's head lolled back and then to the side as he said something to me with a goofy grin. I couldn't hear the remark, but I laughed anyway.

We were coming up fast on an eighteen wheeler truck rumbling along the highway ahead of us. My foot pushed down even harder on the gas.

Somewhere inside my head I was screaming. *No. Stop. Don't let it happen again.* But my body moved without any heed. I couldn't force the thoughts from my scattered mind through my nerves to my limbs.

I'd forgotten how brief the moment of the tragedy had

actually been. The space of a breath, of a few heartbeats. We tore past the truck and jerked back into the lane just as another sedan made a left-hand turn out of a side-road.

I'd been going way too fast to slow down enough, even if my reflexes hadn't been so burned out it barely occurred to me to shift my foot to the brake. It was a blink, the screech of tires, and the wrenching crunch of smashing steel as our Toyota T-boned the other car smack in the middle.

I slammed forward, my seatbelt cracking a rib, the blast of the airbag bruising a few more. One tiny habit left over from all the times my parents had drilled safety practices into me in childhood. No one else in our car had their seatbelts on.

Even through the blaze of pain that wracked my body in that first instant, I registered the shattering of the windshield, the thud of thrown bodies, a strangled cry from someone in the other car. *They*—father, mother, and two young kids, like an echo of my own family ten years ago—all had their belts on, but that didn't help you much when a ton and a half of steel moving faster than it was ever really meant to go slammed right into the middle of the vehicle you were riding in.

In reality, I'd fainted from the shock and pain. The drugs shivering through my system probably hadn't helped my mental state. The next thing I'd been aware of was the jostling of a stretcher I'd been strapped to as frantic paramedics loaded it into an ambulance. I hadn't seen the wreckage or the bodies until I'd found the photos on newscasts and the internet days later—and then, more vividly, when the counseling room had thrown the scene at me on a life-size scale.

None of that compared to actually being here. To tasting the blood where my lip had split, feeling the ache through my cheekbones, as I raised my head and realized this time I was still conscious. The vision hadn't knocked me out—it hadn't wanted to.

I knew without questioning it that no ambulance or other rescuers were coming. This was a private replay just for me, and Roseborne would want me to experience every detail of it I could without interruption.

The airbag deflated enough that I could turn and shove open my door. I staggered out onto the suddenly silent highway.

Somewhere in the back of my head I'd started to think I'd gotten the one small mercy of experiencing this catastrophe alone. But the first thing I saw as I emerged was Trix standing on the side of the highway in the overgrown grass just beyond the gravel shoulder, her orange hair flicking this way and that in the warm but sharp wind, her pale green eyes shadowed. Of course the vision had deposited her right here, where she could have a front-row seat to the carnage.

I couldn't stand to say anything to her now any more than I had when Kadri's ghost had been approaching me. Feeling as though a line of knots had been tied through my organs from throat down to gut, I turned to take in the horrific scene I'd created.

All other vehicles that would have been on the highway had vanished. This might as well have been the only patch of reality left in the entire universe. Mom's Toyota had swung to the side with the impact, the hood crumpled and jagged pieces of windshield glass glinting around the frame. The other sedan looked as if a giant had punched it through the middle, both of the left-hand doors mashed inward, bumpers twisted, windows hollowed.

Kadri lay on the pavement several feet away. I only knew it was him because of his neon green T-shirt. The entire upper half of his head had bashed open, scrambled blood and brains leaking onto the road. A stench like raw meat mixed with tar filled my nose, and nausea surged up. I doubled over and gagged, stomach acid searing my mouth.

The two guys we'd been hanging out with were still in the car, flung against the front seats and the roof, bodies bent and broken. I glanced at them, cringed, and forced myself to step closer to the other car.

How the fuck did I dare to even continue living if I turned my back on the consequences of my screw-ups— the consequences so many people other than me had ended up paying?

I couldn't even make out the father or the kid in the booster seat who'd been on the left side of the car. Well, I could see the ragged stump of an arm here, a splatter of blood and gristle there, but essentially they'd been pulverized on impact.

The crumpled metal had bashed all the way into the mother and the older kid, pummeling them into the far doors. Blood coated their faces where their skulls had cracked open; their bodies sat twisted at warped angles no living being could have tolerated.

My stomach lurched again. I hunched over and spat more acid onto the pavement. There was nothing else in there to come up, but my gut kept churning as if trying to work more free. As if maybe if it wrenched hard enough, I could start puking up my lungs and kidneys and spleen to satisfy that urge. Why the hell shouldn't I, when everyone else here had lost theirs?

There was no one else alive here except Trix, who wasn't meant to be here at all. Who could I apologize to? How could I make up for this, even by a fraction?

How would she ever look at me from now on without seeing blood and broken bones?

I sank closer to the ground and dropped my head to my knees. The stink closed in around me, overwhelming all my other senses.

There *wasn't* anything else I could do. That was the worst part of the whole thing. I could never bring the lives I'd destroyed back. I could never repay what I owed them. I couldn't even come close. Roseborne didn't need to tell me that, but I guessed it wanted to rub the fact in.

My breath seeped from my mouth slow and ragged. My eyes started to burn. I'd just stay here, then. That was what Roseborne's spirits wanted, wasn't it? For me to recognize that there was no undoing what I'd done, and so I should take whatever punishment they threw at me. Even if it was spending whatever time I had left surrounded by my most brutal crime.

Footsteps rasped across the pavement. I held back a flinch and forced myself to raise my head, just slightly.

"Don't," I said.

Trix stopped by the median line. She looked down at the ground and back at me, her mouth twisting. How could she know what to say?

"You can go," I said. "You should. Now you know what kind of scum I was. This is my mess to live with, and I should have to live with it."

"Ryo…" Her voice came out softer than I had any right to expect. "I'm not going to tell you it isn't horrible. But I want to be here with you anyway. Take as much time as you want, but when you're ready—whatever you need, I'll do my best to help."

The question quavered up my throat. "Why?"

She smiled, pained but genuine. "Because I believe in you. I believe you're more than this, even if Roseborne thinks differently."

How could she look around us and still say that? How could she see anything other than a totally wretched human being? I ached to collapse into the ground and offer up all the agony this body could contain…

But that wouldn't fix anything either, would it? Trix was standing there, ready to take action, and what the hell was I doing? Wallowing in my emotions, letting them dictate what I did instead of tackling them and moving myself in a new, better direction. Just like I'd let the drugs and my hunger for them overwhelm every other motivation for years before.

Giving myself over to misery and guilt wasn't any

more noble than chasing a high. I knew that; I'd been trying to pull myself out of that habit, but being thrust into the middle of this scene had nearly pulled me right back down to bottoming out.

My body balked. I hesitated and then pushed myself slowly to my feet. My stomach still listed and that awful smell still choked me, but I couldn't dwell on that.

What did I wish I'd done back then? What did I wish I'd done before the crash had ever even happened?

A tremor of energy passed through my chest as an image sprang into my mind. Yes. By all the gods there were, yes. Even if it wasn't what the vision wanted from me, that was what I needed. I was abruptly sure that if I just concentrated and *pulled* with my will and resolve…

Our surroundings spun around us. The ground lurched, and with an audible snap, Trix and I were standing not amid highway wreckage but in my bedroom in my parents' home. Trix blinked, staring around her in confusion.

I dove straight for my dresser. Boxers and socks tumbled over the edge of the drawer as I dug through them. My fingers closed around the rounded end of a glass pipe. I yanked it out and whipped it at the floor.

The glass burst apart with a smash that sent a pulse of satisfaction and certainty through me. Yes, yes, yes. This was right. Turn all this shit into the garbage it was.

I spun toward the closet and pawed through the mess on the floor to find the smaller pipe I'd hidden there. The shattering of the burnt glass gave me the same relief. I knelt down by the bed, heedless of the shards cracking under my knees, and yanked out the box that held my current stash of powder.

The fine white crystals glinted faintly within the plastic baggie. I snatched it up and charged into the hallway. Trix followed at my heels. She didn't say anything, only bore witness as I marched into the bathroom. Without a second's hesitation, I upended the bag over the toilet. Then I flushed, watching the substance that had directed so much of my life whirl down the drain.

A ragged laugh tumbled out of me. It was gone. It'd been that easy.

Trix tucked her hand around mine. "I guess you didn't need my help after all. You handled it all on your own."

I tugged her closer to me, wanting her warm clementine scent to wash away any lingering traces of the highway stench. "Not all on my own," I said tightly. "Not really. And you're not alone either. I'm here for *you* too, Trix. I believe in you. Whatever's left to face, I know we'll make it through."

My heart thumped with the truth of those words, which sparked a surge of joy in turn. A sharper, starker joy than I'd been able to feel since I'd stepped past Roseborne's gate. I wanted to cling onto it and her with both hands, but as she tipped her head toward me, the vision hurled us both back into darkness.

# CHAPTER TWENTY-ONE

*Trix*

Falling back into the college foyer left me momentarily dizzy after the intensity of Ryo's crash and his destruction of the tools of his addiction. I teetered on my feet in the dimmer golden light cast by the chandelier, and Jenson caught my arm to help me keep my balance.

The four of us were all still together by the base of the grand staircase. Elias was frowning at something by the doorway behind me.

"Trix," he said in a cautious tone.

As I turned, I glanced at Ryo to confirm he'd returned from that agonizing trip through his past all right. The quick, grateful flash of his smile reassured me as much as the memory of his last words there did. *I believe in you.*

One of Roseborne's founding spirits had flitted into the foyer after us. I tensed automatically at the sight of the shining figure streaking from one end of the room to the other. Did they plan to blast us apart again? Could we stop them this time?

But no other bolts of supernatural glow followed this one. When it slowed to a halt in front of me, I recognized Mildred's face amid the light. She peered at me with her lips pursed in a way that fit her former persona as Professor Hubert better than the teenaged girl she appeared as now. As her gaze traveled over me, I got the sense that, like before, it wasn't exactly me she was looking for.

"What do you want?" I asked, briskly but trying to avoid sounding outright hostile. Of the seven, Mildred was the one I'd gotten through to the most. She cared about Winston, and she knew I had a connection to him. If surviving Roseborne was going to require tackling its "staff" head-on, she was still my best hope.

She cocked her head, meeting my eyes directly now, and then hesitated. After a moment, she ventured, "You said you've seen Winston's memories—that you've experienced what he was feeling before, when… everything happened. Does that include what he was doing out there when he decided not to come back?" She motioned a translucent hand to the side to indicate the world beyond the campus.

"No," I admitted. "All the memories of his that have come to me are from here at Roseborne. But that doesn't mean I can't tell from what he was going through then and what I've sensed now that—"

"I know," she said quickly. "I'm not asking so I can

argue. I… I wondered if you'd let me see if we can find those later memories, if I could take a peek inside your head."

Jenson stirred, glowering at her. "Forget that. Do you think we've forgotten who you are and what you've done to us, especially Trix?"

She scowled at him. "I *could* delve inside her mind without asking permission. You should know we've done that plenty of times to all of you in the past." Her gaze slid back to me. "But it'll be easier and more comfortable if you're assisting rather than fighting me. And… I think you and he deserve at least that respect. He was one of us, before."

It was clearly difficult for her to offer me even that minor concession. And I couldn't deny that *I* was curious what had changed my probable great-grandfather's mind too. If whatever had happened had been enough to make him want to break free from Roseborne's toxicity, maybe it would do the same for his former friend.

"How do we know that's all you'll do?" Elias asked, stepping over to me. Ryo closed ranks with us too as if I needed a full guard. Which, to be fair, I might.

Mildred kept her attention focused on me. "Either you trust me or you don't. You wanted to make me see his perspective before. What better way than this?"

My body still stiffened at the idea of the intrusion, but I shoved that resistance down. Winston had cared about this girl once, if not as much as she'd hoped for. I didn't sense any concern from whatever of his essence still resided inside me.

I looked to the guys. I couldn't jump in without offering them some kind of explanation. "We've only gotten this far because of the risks we've been willing to take—the trust we gave each other without any guarantees. There never are any real guarantees. I think I should offer her a chance."

Ryo's mouth tightened, but he nodded.

"You're completely sure?" Jenson said, still eyeing Mildred as if he could ward off any evil intent with the power of his stare.

"We've been running mostly in circles. I want to go forward."

Elias let out a strained breath, but he didn't argue. "You're the only one who can decide what you're prepared to handle, Trix. We'll be right here to help if it looks like you need it."

"Okay." I inhaled deeply and stepped toward Mildred. "Let's do this. I want to see too."

She reached toward me like the lesser ghosts did, but to touch my head rather than my chest. As her fingers seeped through my scalp with a tingling, my mind rose up and away into the same clouded realm as when I'd grabbed her and slipped into her memories earlier tonight.

Flickers of images blinked past me—Winston in this foyer, Winston with the bow and arrows, Winston transforming into a stately middle-aged man who strode through a classroom I'd never entered before with his narrow chin held high.

Then the school fell away. A young man who walked like his teenaged self but looked more filled out and darker haired strode along a street in a city I didn't recognize. Now he stopped in a park, watching groups of friends chattering. Now he was wandering a regular college campus, pausing and fading out of view to listen in on discussions here and there. From the clothes of the people he passed, I guessed this was sometime in the 1950s.

I watched all of the scenes that wavered by from above like I had with Mildred's memories, but Winston's emotions trickled through me in a way hers hadn't, as if part of me were inside him too. Boredom and uncertainty and confusion came in wafts. Then a spark of anger lit as he watched a few of the college students taking turns belittling a young woman in their midst. A ripple of supernatural energy coursed around him—was that the way that he started to lock onto a potential target for Roseborne?

It never developed any further than that ripple, though. A moment later, another young woman with bronze-brown hair like my mother's marched over to the group.

"You all need to get your heads out of your asses," she announced with her hands on her hips. "Do you think it makes you look important when you're happily tearing someone down? Because you really just look pathetic."

A couple of the guys in the group swore at her and the other girls muttered, but the woman who'd intruded didn't show any sign that she cared. She motioned the bullied girl away from the group with a beckoning gesture and led her to a nearby café. Winston watched them go with a heady warmth I could tell he didn't totally understand spreading through his chest. He waited a few seconds, and then he walked after the two girls.

I sensed Mildred beside me then, with a twinge of sorrow that ran through the air between us. When I squinted, I could make out the faintest outline of her form, watching all this as I was. My stomach twisted.

How was *she* going to handle seeing the guy she'd crushed on for decades falling for some other woman? This plan could totally backfire—she might come out of it even more furious at the world than she'd been before.

But we were here now. The images shuddered and jolted forward in time in fits and starts as Mildred must have propelled the memories on in her search for answers. We saw Winston sitting in a different café with the bronze-haired girl across from him, his heart swelling with affection at her easy-going remarks. Saw them hand-in-hand holding signs at some sort of protest. Saw Winston gazing out an apartment window with a pensive expression and a pang of guilt in which I could taste Roseborne's influence before his girlfriend came over and tucked her arm around him, and his distress melted into joy.

When a memory of their wedding day swam up before us, I glanced toward my impression of Mildred's presence again. How was she coping so far? I could *feel* how Winston's connection with this woman had healed his soul and given him new life—could Mildred recognize how deeply it had affected him while watching from the outside?

It   warmed   my   own   heart,   witnessing   his

transformation, but she might view this as nothing more than a betrayal.

Had he ever told his wife—my great-grandmother, I was now more sure than ever—anything about his past? I couldn't imagine how he'd have explained the supernatural aspect of it in any way she'd have believed, but the bullying, the violence… That was a huge secret to carry.

Maybe that was why some part of his spirit had stayed with the family through the generations even after his death, whenever that had been. Why he'd come back here with me. To make his own amends? To carry out some final business with his co-conspirators?

I wished he could just tell me what the hell he wanted here and how I could help make it happen.

The happy couple danced at their reception. "Mildred?" I said tentatively, my voice faint and hollow in the mist that framed the memory. I couldn't tell if she heard me or not. I drew in a breath to try again—

And with a lurch, her presence tore away from me. A second later, I spun out of the realm of memories too, finding myself landing on my butt on the foyer floor, my mind reeling from the abrupt departure.

"Trix!" Ryo dropped down beside me. Elias and Jenson flanked me, and we all stared at the light show happening before our eyes.

The other spirits of Roseborne had congregated just inside the front door. They whirled past Mildred's form like shooting stars. Oscar loomed over her, his glow blazing around him. I could tell from the fury in his stance that he'd yanked her out—and me with her.

Mildred had obviously reached the same conclusion. "What was that about?" she snapped at him. "I wasn't finished with her."

"You should be finished with *him*." Oscar floated higher as if that would intimidate her more. "He showed his true colors ages ago. He's *nothing* to us. He never deserved to be part of Roseborne to begin with."

"I needed to see it for myself. I needed to understand."

"You need to remember who's worked with you all these years. Who helped you get the power that keeps you going."

I scrambled to my feet with the guys' help. Oscar's tone and words left me with an uneasy sense of recognition. It stirred up echoes of times with Cade.

Maybe my foster brother fit in here in ways I'd never even considered.

"We were there for you too," Mildred shot back, her own glow flaring brighter. "You couldn't have gotten what you wanted on your own. You made all those promises for your benefit as much as ours—don't think I can't see that."

Oscar bared his teeth. "If you think *you* have any grounds to complain about—"

Something shifted inside me, a quiver and a jab provoked by what I saw in the leader of the spirits, the way it resonated with my own memories, and its ties to the essence of a boy in me who'd lived under that domineering presence before. A prickling sensation crawled up my throat. I started to swallow it down in an instinctive panic, but caught myself.

No. I'd wanted Winston to speak clearly. Let's see what he could say.

My lips parted, and a voice that didn't sound quite like my own carried from my mouth.

"You can be better than this, Mildred. We can all be better than *him*. We should have been, back then… I wish I'd seen how he was twisting us sooner, before it was too late."

Mildred's head jerked around. She gaped at me, but I knew it wasn't really me she was seeing.

"Winston?" she murmured.

"It can be so much better," his voice said through me. "He has no real hold over you, not if you don't let him."

"Why, you—" Oscar started, lunging toward me with a sharper burst of light and, within it, an unfurling of the dark cloud I'd seen inside him before.

Before he could do whatever he'd meant to, Mildred threw herself between us. "I'm done with you! I'm done with all of this!"

She shoved him backward, and in the same motion her spirit crackled apart like a firework. The glow sprayed all through the room in a shower of sparks, softly warm where they brushed my skin. In their wake, a puddle of shadow dropped to the ground, where it shriveled into nothingness in the time it took for me to blink.

Oscar let out a wordless sound of rage. The other spirits raced back and forth around him with a distress that washed over my skin. Elias grasped my shoulder, Ryo my hand. I might have tugged them and Jenson back up the stairs to get away from whatever fresh hell our captors were about to unleash when the front door burst open.

I hadn't been paying attention to the time. It must have just turned half past midnight. Cade strode into the foyer looking like himself, like the boy I'd grown up with —and at the same time, terrifyingly determined as his gaze fixed on me.

*Trix*

Roseborne's spirits wavered to the side as if to watch what would happen between Cade and the four of us. Two of the brilliant lights streaked away—I wasn't watching closely enough to note which ones. All my attention was focused on the guy in front of me.

The hastily bandaged wounds on my forearm and calf stung with the memory of how I'd gotten them. Jenson had tensed beside me, no doubt starkly conscious of his recent tangle with my foster brother's monstrous form.

Cade looked pretty monstrous even right now, standing on two feet with totally human features. His gray eyes glinted with a furious light, and the muscles all through his broad shoulders and wiry arms flexed against his Henley shirt. His hands had formed fists at his sides. Aggression hummed off his stance.

I didn't for a second believe he was incapable of hurling himself at me or any of the guys the way he had Richie or his dad or any of the other people he'd gotten into altercations with over the years—more than I knew, clearly.

"These assholes are the ones you want to throw your lot in with instead of me?" he said, his voice low and taut. "You think they haven't done at least as much shit as I have? I've looked out for you, taken care of you, for *years*. How can you even compare that, Trix?"

My throat had closed up. I forced myself to speak, even though the anger that had fueled my words in the shed no longer burned as hot. More than anything, faced with the boy who'd been my whole world for so much of my life, I simply felt sad.

"It isn't really taking care of someone if you're going to hold it over their head so they'll do what you want," I said. "And no, I'm not going to tell you anyone in this room is perfect. I've seen how fucked up their lives were too. Just like mine was fucked up. The difference is that they've all been able to do something different since then. You're still treating me like you own me."

His eyes flashed. "I've never said that. And what have they done that's so amazing in the last few months? You couldn't even remember them most of that time."

"While you were so busy preserving your ego that you wouldn't reach out to me at all, even though you knew I was here for you?" I retorted. "They've answered my questions; they've pitched in when I couldn't handle all the parts of a plan on my own; they've encouraged me to figure out my own way instead of trying to force their ideas on me. They've let me decide when I'm ready to take our relationship further. They've acted like my happiness was at least as important as theirs. You've said a lot about how much I matter to you over all those years, but I don't think you've put it into practice as much as they've managed to in a hell of a lot less time."

Elias's hand squeezed my shoulder reassuringly. I suspected he'd have stepped between me and Cade if I'd made any gesture suggesting I wanted his protection, but from the tension in his stance, I could tell he was still struggling just to hold his posture straight.

Roseborne had already worn him down more than I could bear. This was my battle to fight, and I'd damn well fight it.

"They've messed with your head, made you think they're the good guys while they laugh behind your back," Cade sputtered. "There's no way, no fucking way—"

At my other side, Ryo shifted forward just an inch. "We haven't tried to make Trix do *anything*. If you think she's so weak that someone could brainwash her that easily, you obviously don't know her anywhere near as well as you want to think. She's the strongest person I've ever met. It's an *honor* to have been along for the ride while she's taken this place on."

"Do you think laying into us some more is going to make her think you're some great catch?" Jenson tossed out. "Please tell me you're not that stupid."

Cade's eyes narrowed. "From the look of those bandages, going up against me didn't work out so well for you last time. Maybe you should stay out of this."

"Why is it I'm not that scared then? Could it be you're not half as menacing as you'd like to be?"

I held up my hand to cut off any more heckling. "None of this is important right now. We *all* need to get out of this school. Who's doing what with who, who cares about who how much—it makes no difference if we die here because of the biggest assholes of them all."

I waved my hand toward the watching spirits. If they objected to my characterization, they didn't show it. The two that had disappeared briefly streaked through the air to rejoin the others. I studied the mass of their glaring lights warily.

"Maybe I think this is more important," Cade said. "Maybe I'd rather deal with this hell another year than watch these three pricks take you away from me. I get to decide that."

My jaw set. "No, you don't. You don't because I didn't belong to you in the first place. They're not taking anything; I'm *going*. And you don't get to decide where I go."

"That's not how this is supposed to work. If it was just the two of us again—if I could make you see—"

His voice broke with a note of pain. Something twisted in his face, so anguished it wrenched at my heart but so furious at the same time that my pulse stuttered. Before I could really prepare, he flung himself at me with a growl that sounded more like the beast than the boy.

His fingers clenched tight around my wrist, sending a fresh ache through my wounded arm. I jerked back instinctively, trying to scramble away, but he yanked me toward him at the same moment. Ryo leapt in, and Cade punched him in the face so hard I heard the crack of bone. Blood gushed from Ryo's nose.

"Stop it!" I said, halfway between my own fury and a surge of panic. "Leave them alone—leave me alone —just—"

The next heave of his hand sent a sear of pain up my arm. My voice cut off with a yelp. I stumbled toward him, Elias rushed in, Cade swung his fist again—

And a blaze of light knocked my foster brother off his feet with an electric crackle that snapped his hold on me and pinned him to the floor on his back. I careened backward into Jenson's arms. As he steadied me, Oscar's glowing figure straightened up over Cade. One of the other spirits, a guy whose name I didn't remember, stayed braced over my foster brother, not so much as wincing at Cade's ineffective struggles.

"He isn't going to stop," Oscar said in a cool voice that reminded me of his demeanor as Dean Wainhouse. "He's going to torment you and attack anyone you care about other than him for as long as he's still alive, out of the love he claims to feel for you. It's the only way he knows how to show that devotion. You can put an end to it, protect yourself and them and everyone else he might hurt, right here, right now."

His ghostly hand lifted with a completely solid knife

in its grasp. A knife I recognized well enough for the sight to chill me.

It was the blade he and his followers had used to slash open their wrists in the final act of the sacrifice of life and blood that had transformed them and this school. The one that he'd shoved into the basement floor in the pool of their blood to grow the demented rosebush I'd destroyed. It'd remained there afterward—he and the other guy must have raced down there to retrieve it for this purpose. He held the weapon out to me now, turning it so I could grasp the wooden handle.

I took it, if only because I'd rather it was in my hand than his. My fingers curled around the grip as if they were meant to be there. Oscar smiled at me encouragingly. On the floor, Cade thrashed against his captor. Another spirit joined them to help him still.

A whiff of supernatural energy quivered from the knife into me. It settled in my chest, cold but potent. I found myself thinking of the glimpses of the ritual I'd seen in Winston's memories. The power those eight students had brought into themselves by sacrificing their blood—and someone else's.

Plenty of my blood had spilled around campus. If I did what Oscar was urging, if I stabbed this blade right into Cade's heart, would I gain enough power to challenge the remaining spirits?

It wouldn't be like what they'd done, not really. One death to prevent dozens of others. The death of a guy who'd already attacked my lovers more than once, who'd made every appearance of aiming to kill Jenson in the shed.

The thought passed through my mind, chillingly smooth—and I shoved it away with a wave of revulsion. The thought of plunging this knife into any part of my foster brother's body brought bile into my throat.

I wasn't a killer. Cade didn't deserve to be treated like a rabid animal. None of this was okay.

I'd found power within me before through other kinds of sacrifice—sacrificing the security of shutting myself off from everyone around me, sacrificing the lies that protected me to offer up the truth of my awful mistakes. If I was going to beat these fiends now, that was how I'd do it, not by buying into their version of the game.

I stepped closer to Cade and raised the knife. He went still, staring up at me. His eyes widened, his mouth forming a stiff line—and then the tightening of his features relaxed with a hopeless sort of resignation. A hopelessness of my own constricted my lungs.

He honestly believed I could do it. That I could turn on him even more utterly than his dad had all those years ago. He might even be thinking it was inevitable. How could I ever hope to get through to him, to be enough that he'd care about me in a way that didn't tie me down, if after all this time he couldn't even trust me that much?

Maybe I couldn't, but that didn't change what I had to do.

"I can't be with you or be there for you the same way I was before," I said to him. "I can't give you everything. But I forgive you for wanting it. Maybe there's a monster in you, and this place has brought it out even more, but that's not all you are. You've also been my brother and my defender and my support system, and I'm never going to forget those things. Even if those parts of what we had are in the past now, they still count."

Oscar's mouth started to move, but before he could speak, I dropped to the ground and plunged the knife into the floorboards. "Grow again," I said, with a flare of power like when I'd owned up to my crimes to the guys behind me. "Grow something better, for me and all of us who are more than our mistakes."

The knife didn't transform, but another, larger surge of energy shot through me.

Cade stared up at me. His expression wavered, puzzled and then filling with something like awe. "Trix," he said hoarsely. "I—I never *wanted* to be—It wasn't—"

Oscar's lips drew back in a snarl as he cut my foster brother off. "Winston had the darkness in him," he said to me. "Winston woke it up and gave it life. It's still in you too. We just have to find the right incentive for you to let it loose." He raised his head to look beyond me. "If anger won't do it, maybe grief will."

At some signal I didn't see, the other spirits launched themselves toward Elias in one mass. I cried out as they crashed into him, slamming him to the ground with a horrible thump. He cast out with his arms and legs to try to fend them off, but there were too many of them. Light blazed across his mouth, around his neck, against his chest —to strangle him or suffocate him or maybe both at once, I didn't know.

I tried to catch hold of them to wrench them off him. Jenson and Ryo—bloody nose and all—jumped in too. But even with the power flowing through me, my hands passed through the spirits' bodies like they were nothing but frigid mist.

A choked gurgling sound escaped Elias. His movements were weakening; his face flushing dark. My eyes flooded. I whipped around to face Oscar, grasping for something, anything that might make him call them off.

It wasn't the ringleader whose gaze I ended up meeting but Cade's. He'd pulled himself to his feet as soon as the spirits had left him. He stood there, swaying slightly, taking in the tears trickling down my cheeks and the despair that must have been etched all over my face.

"Trix," he murmured, his voice even more ragged. "No."

I had no idea what he was saying no to. His gaze slid to Elias under the barrage of spirits and back to me. His jaw clenched. Then in a surge of motion, he snatched the knife from where I'd stabbed it into the floor and dove into the fray.

My ragged protest echoed his. "No!" But even as the syllable broke from my throat, I realized he wasn't joining in the attack. He was slashing not down toward Elias but left and right into the spirits that were wringing the life from the other guy.

"Get off him, you bastards!" he shouted. "She's been hurt enough already."

He was defending Elias for *me*. And his efforts were

working. The spirits flinched away when the blade cut through them. Elias managed to suck in a rough breath.

Jenson, Ryo, and I rushed back in, grasping Elias's shoulders and hands, hauling him away from the glowing menace. The spirits were now whirling up around Cade instead. They jerked this way and that around his swings of the knife, blazing more fiercely by the second.

Then the brightest bolt of all seared into their midst. Oscar wrenched the knife from Cade's hands. He moved to lunge past my brother, the blade aimed at us. With a wordless sound of protest, Cade hurled himself between the spirit and our cluster.

Oscar's hand slammed down. He drove the knife with all his might into my brother's chest.

Cade sagged and toppled over on the floor. I let out a breathless shriek. As Jenson and Ryo guided Elias the rest of the way to the stairs, I ran to my brother.

The spirits backed away, watching again with that sickening curiosity. The blaze of their light drained away into something much paler. My hands clenched as I knelt next to Cade.

He was still breathing in short rasps, blood flecking his lips. More of that liquid crimson was spreading across his shirt far too fast for me to believe I had any hope of saving him. His hand fumbled to the side and managed to grasp mine. His voice rattled as it left his mouth.

"I love you, Trix. Always did, always will. But I never really gave you a chance to be what I needed, did I? Fucked it up way too much. You—you deserve better."

"Cade. You didn't have to—"

He coughed wetly and managed a sickly smile. "If I stuck around, I'd probably go back to fucking us up all over again. I can already feel— This way, it works out. You can keep fighting, and you don't lose the guy who made you look that upset. I won't be able to go back on the one good thing I've done for you here."

Fresh tears sprang to my eyes. "I didn't want you *dead*."

Cade's smile softened. "Best way I could have gone," he said, barely a whisper. His body shuddered.

His fingers slipped from mine. His eyes rolled back. They stayed there, unblinking, as his chest stilled.

I swiped at my eyes, gasping around a sob. A shudder to match Cade's rippled through the spirits surrounding us. As I looked up at them, their light dimmed even more. The darkness twining through them shone more prominently, as if leaching their energy away. At the same moment, a glow expanded inside me, sharp and heady enough to cut through my grief.

Cade had done more for me, for all of us, than he'd even realized. He'd sacrificed his own life—not out of vengeance, but out of love. And the power of that act was singing through me even as it diminished the spirits who'd held us here. That was why they'd drawn back, why they'd pulled away from the fight.

They were scared of *me* now.

The agony inside me solidified with a sense of purpose. I couldn't bring my brother back, but I could make his death mean something. A certainty gripped me that if I marched out of here in this moment, I could blast straight through the gate and free us all.

I grasped Cade's hand one last time and ducked quickly to brush a kiss to his forehead. "Thank you," I murmured, choking up all over again. Then, despite my heavy heart, I pushed myself upright. In the face of my glare, the spirits twitched backward.

"Come on," I called back to the other three guys. "We're getting out of Roseborne right now—all of us."

# CHAPTER TWENTY-THREE

*Elias*

With Jenson's and Ryo's help, I managed to stand. My legs wobbled, and my throat ached from the way the spirits had battered it, but I could hold my own weight for at least a little while longer. I could breathe. And seeing Trix lit up with a glow that rivaled that of the ghosts gave me even more strength.

If she could keep going after the catastrophe and loss she'd just experienced, if she could find the will to fight even harder, then I'd be damned if I let myself falter.

She glanced back at us, the supernatural light gleaming in her eyes as well. I nodded to say I'd follow.

We walked together out the front door with her in the lead. As I passed Cade's limp body, conflicted emotions squeezed my chest. I hadn't wanted that guy anywhere near Trix after I'd found out how he'd treated her, but I wouldn't have said he deserved to die either. He'd still meant something to her—I believed her when she said he wasn't a total monster.

Hell, he'd proved that to me more than anyone just now. If he hadn't intervened, I'd probably be the one sprawled lifeless in the foyer.

Outside, the cool night air washed over us, giving me the sense of being wiped clean. I'd meant to go with Trix all the way to the gate. But as I came down the front steps, tensing the muscles in my thighs to hold myself steady, one more ghost came wavering across the lawn toward me.

A ghost in the shape of my grandfather.

My legs locked completely. My first instinct was to reach into my suit jacket pockets for whatever brambles I had left that might deflect him. My fingers closed around the broken twigs and thorns—and they crumbled away into dust at my touch.

Apparently that protection came with an expiration date.

He was gliding toward me faster now. I couldn't have outrun him in my current state even if I'd wanted to abandon Trix and the others. If I had to do this, I'd better get it over with quickly so I could be here for her when it mattered the most.

I touched Ryo's shoulder just long enough to get his attention. "Go," I said, not leaving any room for argument. "I'll come as soon as I can." Then, squaring my shoulders, I pushed myself forward to meet the old man.

He had the same cold expression I'd been met with so often during my childhood. In some ways, living under his rule had been like living here at Roseborne—a place of perpetual cloud where the slightest rays of sunlight or moonshine beaming down became something precious. I'd gotten enough warmth to manage to grow, even if my perspective had ended up warped in ways I hadn't realized until too late. Was it any wonder my sister had gone off the rails when he'd iced her out so thoroughly from her first reckless moments as a little kid?

That was the last thought that passed through my head, and then he grabbed me, wrenching me from the darkness beyond Roseborne's mansion through a dizzying whirl and out into the stately atmosphere of his apartment's dining room.

With a jolt up my spine, I dropped into the chair where I'd always sat. The antique clock in the corner ticked; the familiar wood polish smell rose off the broad mahogany table and the matching sideboard and china cabinet.

Between the furniture and trimmings, this place echoed the college's vibe more than I'd remembered. My grandfather had always wanted to build his history in this country backward as well as forward, as if the trappings of old money would deepen his roots and make them even more unshakeable.

He paced the floor on the other side of the table now, like he always had when he'd been displeased with me. That was the ritual: I sat here, and he lectured me until he'd unloaded all the frustrations and demands provoked by whatever misstep I'd made, no matter how small.

How old had I been the last time that had happened?

Shortly after I'd moved out into my own apartment at nineteen? He'd had fewer opportunities after that… but mostly I'd been so indoctrinated by his views that I'd given him very few reasons to feel he needed to.

Not now. Now he turned toward me with a fearsome expression that would have set my pulse thumping twice as hard when I'd been in elementary school. Even at twenty-five years old, I couldn't stop my heart from stuttering briefly.

He rapped his cane against the floor. I didn't think he actually needed the thing to help him walk—he'd taken it up several years ago mostly because he liked the intimidating gestures he could make with it. I'd never seen him carry it outside the apartment. It was to make statements to us. He wouldn't want to risk any stranger thinking him weak because of it.

"What do you have to say for yourself?" he asked in his brutally commanding tone. "You really couldn't have made more of a mess of things, could you? Have you forgotten everything I ever taught you?"

I also couldn't fend off the frigid wave of shame that pummeled me in the wake of that tone and those words. Four and a half years without seeing him, of realizing how much his style of "parenting" had screwed me up, and all it took was a few seconds for him to cut right through me again.

I had to stay focused. Trix might need me out there in the real world—and the last thing she needed was to get distracted trying to help me. I was going to get out of this vision on my own, and fast.

"What are you talking about?" I said, managing to bring out the smooth voice I'd cultivated for business meetings and negotiations. "I followed the principles you taught me to the letter. You can't really be complaining about that."

He jabbed his forefinger at me. "You've let yourself become weak. Let others get the better of you and take charge over you. No DeLeon should accept that."

"I've been biding my time," I said, putting the situation in terms I knew he'd respond better to. "When your opponents have more power than you, sometimes you need to wait and pick your battles rather than go charging in. Wouldn't you have told me that?"

My grandfather ignored that point. He started to pace again with sharp strikes of his cane against the floor. "And now you've tied yourself to this *girl*. What prospects does she have? What could she possibly want from you except to leech off your success and security? You've let your heart go too soft, making stupid decisions like your sister did."

My temper flared beneath the cool I'd been keeping. How dare he talk about Trix like that? How dare he talk about *Gloriana* like that?

My hands started to clench under the table, but I forced them to relax. He wouldn't respect anger. If I lost my cool, he'd only sneer at me more.

"I don't know what you mean by 'tied to.' I've enjoyed her company. She's helped me become stronger, not weaker. And she's become the key to getting out of this mess you're so upset that I'm in, so it'd be stupid *not* to stand with her. I'm thinking of my own best interests here."

He scoffed. "A boy's excuses for following his dick rather than his brain. You think I can't tell the difference? Maybe it's best that this place swallowed you up. Spared me having to find out what a disappointment you'd turn out to be too."

My face flushed, shame and anger warring in my chest. This was taking too long already. Why couldn't I find the right words to free myself from this scenario? It'd always been difficult to convince my grandfather of anything he didn't already agree with, but I knew him through and through. I should be able to come up with a strategy that would change his mind—

Unless that wasn't the point.

I studied him for a moment across the table as that idea sank in. The other visions I'd experienced and that Trix had talked about—those had been about making amends. What amends did I need to make with my grandfather, really? If anything, *he* should be apologizing for the mistakes he'd made raising *me*.

I'd let myself get wrapped up in trying to meet his approval all over again, even as I was arguing with him. Who the fuck cared what he thought of my tone now? Whether I could get him to agree with my decisions? They were *mine*, damn it, and that was all he needed to know about it.

With a scrape of the legs against the floorboards, I pushed back my chair and stood up. My grandfather jerked to a halt, his eyes widening just slightly. I'd never dared to interrupt one of his tirades anywhere near so blatantly.

"Fine," I said, setting my hands on the table. "Be disappointed in me. I don't give a shit either way. *I* know that I'm doing the right thing for me, and it's my life, so my opinion matters a hell of a lot more than yours."

He started to sputter. "You're barely done being a boy. You have no idea what you're talking about. Throwing your elders' judgment back in their faces—"

I let my anger flow through me, stirring up a deeper sense of resolve. "Yeah, I will throw it back at you. You shaped me every step of the way from when I was four years old. If you can't trust that the useful parts of those lessons have stuck with me after all that time, then clearly you don't think very highly of yourself either. I've listened enough. Now it's time for me to pay attention to what I want. What I need."

"Oh, and what have you made of yourself striking out on your own? Your company fell apart without you; you've got nothing to show for all that work. If you ever do make it out of that place, you'll be nothing but a loser and a failure."

To my surprise, I found I could laugh at that insult. The sound felt good vibrating up from my lungs, as if it'd cracked through a shell I hadn't known was keeping part of my emotions locked tight.

"I won't be a failure," I said. "Because I'll have beat not just the assholes keeping us down at Roseborne but also your badgering in my head. You held me back in so many more ways than you helped me. I don't need all this junk that you tried to convince me made me more worthy than anyone else."

I yanked at my suit jacket, designer label and tailored to fit, and tossed it on the table. The Rolex he'd encouraged me to buy, that I hadn't seen since I'd entered Roseborne, encircled my wrist. I unlatched it and threw it away with the jacket. Just like that, my body had gotten ten times lighter.

"You ungrateful bastard of a—" my grandfather raged.

"You're the ungrateful one," I shot back before he could continue. "You never appreciated how hard I worked to meet your approval. And you're the loser. Because you know the one good thing that's come out of this hellish situation? I realized what's really important, and that's not how much money you make or how many employees are working under you. It's the people you care about who care about you. Those people matter more than anything. And if you lose sight of that, you lose yourself. It's too bad you forgot that, if you ever knew it, way too long ago."

As my words rang out into the air, the vision around me shattered apart. I plummeted through a rush of wind and darkness back to the stiller darkness of Roseborne's night.

The conversation that had felt so agonizing in the moment must have taken nearly no time at all in reality. Trix was still striding across the lawn toward the gate, the other two guys right behind her, but as I caught my balance, she slowed. A moment later, I saw why.

A ghostly image of a teenaged girl was drifting across the grass to meet her, eyes narrowed accusingly and face tight with rage. Roseborne's ghosts weren't done with Trix yet.

# CHAPTER TWENTY-FOUR

*Trix*

I hadn't really forgotten what—or rather, who—had been waiting for me by the gate. I'd just let myself not think about it for as long as I could. The second Sylvie's form glided into view, my ribs seemed to clench around my lungs, while a sense of resignation radiated through the rest of my body.

Maybe I'd gotten through to Cade when it had mattered most, even if I hadn't been able to save him. Maybe I had the power to challenge the spirits who ran this school now. But I still couldn't outrun the worst parts of my past. My reckoning wasn't over, and I couldn't save anyone else until I dealt with my own crimes.

"Trix?" Jenson said, shooting me a questioning look. "Do you think we can divert her?"

She was coming up on me too fast. I took a step back but didn't let myself move any farther than that. "I've got to see this through. I owe her as much as I owe anyone here." I owed her more, really. "I don't know how long it'll take. In the meantime, can you call everyone who's still here and alive to come to the gate? Send someone to help Violet down from the dorms if you can, assuming she's still there. We might need to get out fast if we want—"

I'd spat out the words as quickly as I could, but Sylvie still caught me before I could finish. My voice wrenched away from me as I hurtled into this final, most awful vision.

My combat boots thumped against the rain-slick pavement. The walls on either side of the alley loomed over me. A breath of cool, damp air flooded my lungs, and my fingers clenched around the leash I'd been gripping.

The dog at the other end of that leash tugged against my hold and let out a low growl. The hairs on the back of my neck and all down my arms stood on end. Any second I was going to hear the tap of Sylvie's shoes approaching—

There they were, sharply staccato against the pavement. I swiveled on my feet, my heart leaping to the base of my throat, looking for a way out, a way to stop this…

I couldn't let the dog go at her. That was what had made her panic—that'd been the key to my horrible plan. If I released him now, he'd probably still run at her. I couldn't approach her while holding him. I didn't think walking away from this encounter would get me out of the vision. Think, Trix.

My gaze fell on a pipe jutting from the side of one of the buildings at knee-level. That would do it. With hasty movements, I hauled the dog back a few feet and tied the leash around the pipe, giving it a tug to make sure the knot was secure. The dog strained against it and let out a huff. One part of this massive problem taken care of.

Sylvie's footsteps stopped. Her voice carried from the courtyard beyond the alley. "Hello? I'm here like you asked."

In that first second, my whole body froze. I didn't want to have to look her in the face, especially not here of all places. I'd spent so much time silently resenting her and feeling usurped by her, but ultimately she'd never hurt me at all. I'd been the only villain between the two of us.

Which was exactly why I knew Roseborne wouldn't be satisfied until I acknowledged that fact to the person who needed to hear it most.

The power that had filled me in the school foyer had fallen away as I'd tumbled into the vision. Walking to meet Cade's former girlfriend, I felt more pathetic than strong. A shiver ran through my body. I crossed my arms over my chest as if I could ward off the chill that way, even though it was coming from inside me rather than out.

Sylvie stood in a streak of light cast by a dim security lamp, her black hair as sleek as ever, perfectly matched with her kohl-lined eyes. Like a slim, mod version of Cleopatra, I'd used to think in my more generous, envious moments. Her thin eyebrows arched when I emerged from the thicker shadows of the alley.

"Beatrix? What are you doing here?"

Behind me, the Rottweiler's claws scrabbled against the ground. I willed him to stay quiet and calm. "I'm the one who asked you to come," I said, managing to keep my voice steady if quiet. "It was—it was a stupid thing. I was going to play a prank on you. And maybe I was hoping you'd get hurt in the process. But I know now—I know how awful that was."

She eyed me warily, her chin coming up. "And I'm supposed to just believe you after you admit something like that? You've always hated me, haven't you? What the hell did I ever do to you?"

*You took away the only person who seemed to really care about me*, I thought but didn't say. The image of Cade collapsed on the floor, the knife in his chest, came back to me with a sickening lurch of my gut—and an unexpected thought.

He'd played with my emotions so I'd always be on my toes, eager to please him however I could. So he could be sure I'd stick with him. He'd dangled affection and withdrawn it when he wanted to maneuver me. Why would I think he'd only operated that way with me? He'd used Sylvie's presence in his life to make me anxious about losing him... How had he used me with her? Was there more to her hostility than I'd provoked?

I took a tentative step farther into the courtyard, careful not to come close enough that she might take my approach as threatening. My mouth had gone dry. I wet my lips.

"I was jealous," I said. "Because a lot of the time Cade used to spend with me, he started spending with you instead. But that was up to him. It's not like you forced him. I should have realized that—I should have looked at how he handled the situation and spoken up to him rather than resenting you."

"Please," Sylvie sneered. "He was constantly running off to take care of you. Sometimes it felt like we couldn't get through one date without him texting you or even taking off. *You* were the problem."

Was that true? I didn't know anything about that, but Roseborne's spirits might, since they'd had access to Cade's memories as well. The queasy sensation inside me bubbled higher.

"I never texted him when he was out with you," I said. "I was too worried about pissing him off by acting needy. If he said it was me he was talking to…"

"Why would he lie?"

After all tonight's conversations with Cade, I knew the answer to that without needing to think much about it, as much as I hated that it was true. "To keep you on the hook. To remind you that he had other girls in his life. He always wanted a little uncertainty so we'd go along with what he wanted when he was giving us his attention. Proving that he could jerk us around was the only way he could feel sure we wouldn't walk away."

Sylvie's lips pursed with a tightness that suggested she recognized that dynamic more than she'd have wanted to. "He really cared about me," she protested. "He was always saying—he was so sweet most of the time."

"Yeah." I knew that side of the equation too. A sudden sense of sisterhood rushed into me.

I'd resented her and, okay, maybe even hated her a

little, and the whole time we'd really been on the same side, dealing with Cade's demons.

"Did he convince you to do things you weren't totally sure you wanted to do?" I found myself asking, even though her answer couldn't be totally real. "Did he make you feel like—like you were letting him down somehow if you ever said no?"

Sylvie winced. "I don't want to talk about that," she said, her voice abruptly rough.

That was enough of an answer. I couldn't really imagine he'd never have used the same tactics on his girlfriend as he had on me. It'd just been easier with me because he'd had so much time to build up my loyalty and dependence.

And I'd blamed her for it.

"I'm sorry," I blurted out, so emphatically my chest ached with the admission. "So fucking sorry."

Her lips twisted into a frown. "It's a little late for that, don't you think? You already stole my whole life away, you bitch. You couldn't have seen what was going on before you went off on your awful crusade?"

Heat burned in my cheeks. "You're right. I should have. I can't be sorry enough. But I don't know what else to say. I'm not asking you to forgive me. You probably shouldn't. I just want you to know that *I* know how wrong it was."

"Well, I'm sorry if I can't bring myself to really care."

The words stung, but I deserved them. I opened my mouth, closed it again, and then ventured, "He's gone."

Sylvie's expression softened with confusion. "Who? Gone where?"

Oh, God. My throat closed up before I managed to work my voice again. "Cade. He—the spirits at Roseborne —he was saving someone else's life. And the spirits killed him for it. Deep down, he wanted to be someone who helped people rather than someone who hurt them. I don't know all the things he had weighing on him… His dad, the foster families we were with… But it wasn't all an act. He cared. I'm sure he cared about you, even if it came out wrong sometimes."

I hadn't realized how much it would sting to admit that last bit. If Cade had gotten himself sorted out in the real world—or even at Roseborne in time to save himself —maybe he'd have come to care about someone like Sylvie more than he had me. And that would have been okay. I didn't have just him anymore either.

The thought of the three guys waiting for me back on campus sent a pang of urgency through me, but I held myself in place. This vision and Sylvie didn't appear to be finished with me yet. What else did they want from me?

Sylvie bit her lip and looked at the ground. I expected her to accuse me of failing Cade or to break down in tears, and I braced myself. But before either of those things could happen, or anything else, my attention was caught by a fresh scraping of clawed paws against the pavement down the alley. A scraping and a snarled bark—and the snap I immediately knew was the breaking of the leash.

Panic flashed through me and across Sylvie's face. A volley of barks carried toward us, louder by the second.

She backed up a step, all the color draining from her face, and started to whirl around.

I leapt to her and caught her by the elbow. "No!" I said raggedly. "That way! Get out of here. I'll cover you."

I shoved her away from the broad glass window she'd crashed through in reality, toward the shorter alley she'd entered the courtyard from. Sylvie fled. I spun around, just in time for the Rottie to come charging into the courtyard.

He lunged to the side, after her, and without a second thought, I threw myself into his way. His massive, muscled body slammed into me like Cade's had in his beast form when I'd first encountered him at Roseborne all those days ago.

I fell, my back smacking the hard ground with a jolt of pain, but all my attention narrowed down to digging my fingers around the dog's neck, catching his collar, holding him here with me no matter how he bit or scratched, until Sylvie could make her escape.

Hot, meaty breath wafted over my face. A heavy paw socked me in the gut. Jaws gnashed by my ear, I clung on to the collar tighter—and all the pieces of the scene flew away from me.

Or rather, I flew away from them, spiraling and falling on my hands and knees on the lawn, no more than ten feet from the gate.

I shoved myself upright as fast as I could. The sense of power that had come over me before shot back through my veins, even more potent than before.

A crowd of students with anxious faces had gathered

by the wall, my three guys in their midst. Elias shot me a relieved smile and then stiffened when his gaze slid past me.

I whirled around. A blast of multiple streaks of light had just burst past the school's doors. Roseborne's spirits had rallied some of their own power. And now they were blazing straight toward me and every person I'd intended to save.

# CHAPTER TWENTY-FIVE

*Trix*

I didn't wait for Oscar and the other vengeful spirits to reach me. With a hitch of my pulse, I whipped around and hurled myself toward the gate. The eerie energy that I'd used to break through the basement wall earlier this evening, to hack apart the twisted rosebush, thrummed through every inch of my body.

I could do this. I just needed to make it there before the spirits reached me.

My combat boots thudded over the lawn. The students standing closest to the gate pulled back to make way, their eyes wide. I barely felt the ground beneath my feet for the last few steps.

My hands slammed into the bars. I grasped the latch and willed all the power inside me into wrenching it open.

With a grating sound, it sprang free. The gate moved

at my heave, swinging open so smoothly a startled but joyful laugh spilled from my mouth.

And then the spirits hit me.

They pummeled me into the swing of the gate with a burning intensity that seared my skin hot enough to sting. My breath hissed through my teeth at the pain. My fingers clasped tightly around the gate's bars as my feet stumbled over the asphalt on the other side. More of that blazing energy shoved at me, forcing both me and the gate farther out.

They were pushing it open even wider? Why would they want *that*?

With the next slam of supernatural force, so hard my hands jarred and nearly broke from the bars, understanding clicked in my head. It wasn't the gate they wanted to push—it was only me. They were trying to propel me right out of the school and away, and then I'd bet they'd yank the gate closed again faster than you could blink. Kick me out, leave everyone else trapped inside. One last-ditch, desperate gambit.

One that might work. Would I be able to open the gate from the outside once I'd left campus? Already the power I'd put into the act was fraying with their battering. Whatever magic Roseborne held, it could seep beyond the campus walls, but maybe not with the same strength.

Then I just had to hold on until there was no one left for them to confine.

"Come on, everyone!" I shouted over the howl of energy around me. "Get out while you can. Don't let them stop you!"

Easier said than done. The spirts whirled and shrieked through the opening. I peeked behind me long enough to see a couple of students make a run for freedom, only to be smacked backward onto their asses.

Sizzling fingers yanked at me. Two of the spirits rammed into me from the side. I skidded a foot farther, one of my hands snapping off the gate for an instant before I snatched at the bars again. A smell like baked cement and ozone, a hot summer day with a thunderstorm brewing, clogged my nose and lungs.

Holding the gate wasn't enough. I had to stop Roseborne's spirits… somehow. What could I do when I could barely hang on right here?

A tall, brawny figure managed to shove past the spirits' blockade at the far end of the gate. Elias hauled himself toward me hand over hand along the bars, planting each step against the bolts of energy that struck at him. As some of the spirits focused on him, Jenson and Ryo managed to follow along the same path.

Blood was leaking through the bandage on Jenson's shoulder, and Ryo's nose had swollen where Cade had punched him, but they all looked so determined I wasn't sure even a tidal wave could have knocked them down. They pressed their shoulders into the gate, holding it open alongside me.

"Did you really think we were going to back down now?" Jenson yelled at the swarm of spirits. "Fuck that."

Ryo's voice joined his. "You'll have to break a lot more than my nose to get rid of me."

Elias's hand closed over mine with a firm squeeze. He

looked at me rather than our enemies. "You do whatever you need to do. We'll keep standing right here with you. This is exactly where I'm meant to be." He hesitated, and his voice dropped so I could barely hear it over the spirits' furious roar. "I love you. I wish I'd said that sooner."

A bittersweet lump filled my throat. If I could have kissed him without risking everything, I would have. I'd have kissed all three of them for taking this stand with me.

That was how we won, wasn't it? Love instead of hate. Forgiveness instead of vengeance. Sacrifice instead of self-preservation. Two long chains of cause and effect unfolded in my mind as the spirits shifted their attention to batter more of the students who attempted to join us.

In some ways, that conflict had made up so much of our lives from the start. Chains of meaning that could be skewed in one direction or the other. There was darkness in me, sure. Darkness that had been left to stew after my parents' abandonment, after the abuse I'd suffered from one foster family and another. Darkness Cade had stoked into something dangerous with his emotional manipulation.

His darkness had been fueled in turn by the battles he'd had to fight, the hurt he'd carried over his parents' beatings and rejection. And who knew what had happened to his mom and dad or mine to lead them down the paths they'd gone down?

Everyone faced pain and betrayals and pressure from people who didn't have their best interests at heart. I'd seen it over and over again in the stories of all the other students here, in the history that had brought this place into being to begin with.

Oscar and the others' need for vengeance hadn't come out of nowhere, after all. It'd been built on the back of the torment their classmates had inflicted on them first. And God only knew what had driven *those* students' animosity, if you kept unraveling the chain further and further back.

But there were paths out of that seemingly endless spiral. Winston had found one in the shape of a woman who'd shown him there were people who would stand up for what was right even when they didn't need to. He'd loved her more than he'd hated the people who'd cut him down here, and that had given him the strength to leave Roseborne for good. To pass on some of his power through the generations until there'd been a time when one of us could use it.

Mildred had freed herself through her love for him and her decision to let go rather than keep attacking us. In some small way, I might have freed Cade with my forgiveness as much as he'd freed himself with his sacrifice. The power that I'd used to open this gate had come with each step I'd taken on that route away from pain and anger, toward compassion and affection.

So, how could I use that now?

The spirits thrashed around in the gate's opening, still managing to block off anyone else who might have tried to escape. Within the disparate streaks of light, that shadowy energy I'd noticed before unfurled in thicker wafts. The sight of it stirred something deep in me with faint flickers of memories and emotions I knew weren't mine.

An awful lot of Winston's essence lived on in me. *He* was looking through me at the people he'd considered his friends. Maybe what they'd done to their classmates and then themselves had ultimately been an act of hate, but he'd been devoted to those seven people too. He'd stuck with them out of a bond of loyalty just like I'd stuck with Cade, until we'd each seen how much more and how much better love could be.

Winston didn't hate them, even now. He… felt sorry for them. It pained him to see them in this distress, still clinging to their old resentments. All that toxicity fueled everything here at Roseborne, from the weather to the life cycles of the roses that clung to this wall.

A tearing sensation formed in my chest, creeping up toward my throat. I resisted instinctively. What would it do to *me* to let go of a life essence that had supported me, given me power? How tightly was what remained of Winston's soul entangled with mine?

I dragged in a breath and found a certainty in myself with the memory of Cade's last words, of the power that had raced through me with them, of the moment when I'd thrown myself in the path of a rampaging dog to save Sylvie's life where I'd ruined it before.

It didn't matter what happened to me. I couldn't live with myself if I put my own survival over trying to set everything here right—and Roseborne kept on killing. So I would follow Winston's tug and the understanding that had come to me, and discover whether I got to live with that or die in the process. One final test. I wasn't sure who it was for most.

I pulled myself back along the gate, past Elias and Jenson and Ryo with a quick squeeze of each of their hands. They braced themselves even more solidly against the asphalt. As I reached the opening, the energy of the rushing spirits shook my hold. A couple of them whirled toward me with a tensing of their faces.

Before they could throttle me again, I sprang the last few feet to the stone wall and the branches of the rosebush climbing it. One hand closed around a handful of leaves and thorns, my skin prickling with drawn blood. The other I held out toward the blazing spirits as if to take their hands in turn.

"He forgives you," I called out to them. "He only ever wanted you to find peace and be safe from the people who hurt you. You can have that now. He'll be right there with you." I swallowed hard. "And I forgive you too. You tortured us the way you were tortured. Let it end here. Let the roses grow free."

My sense of Winston's presence expanded inside me. I closed my eyes. "Go and do what *you* need to do," I whispered to him. "I won't stop you."

With the last rush of power thrumming through me, I opened myself up—body, mind, and spirit. Winston broke away from me with a pain that seared from my forehead to my gut. I cried out, but it was a release as much as a wound, a brilliance that flashed behind my eyelids and streamed from my hands toward the friends he'd given so much for and then given up, toward the brambles tied to the lives of every student who'd entered this college.

My legs sagged. For a few seconds, my senses dulled. I wasn't aware of anything except the energy streaming through me and out of me. My knees hit the ground, and the impact jarred my eyes open.

Roseborne's spirits were still racing this way and that beside me, but the shadows I'd seen inside them were fracturing apart. The darkness disintegrated into a haze that blew away from them like dust. Their light faded, but not exactly dwindling. It simply spread out farther, stretching across the lawn to the mansion and the other buildings, out along the wall, and up toward the starred sky.

A warmth tingled through the section of rosebush I was still clutching. Someone in the crowd of students still gathered around the gate sucked in an awed breath. I leaned forward to see fresh blooms bursting open all along the wall, filling the air with a fresh scent that held no hint of decay.

My fingers slipped away from the brambles. I sank to my hands and knees, but my vision stayed steady. My heart thumped with all the power it needed to keep going; my lungs drew in air.

Winston had left me, had given what life he still had to the campus and his former friends, and I'd survived it.

My three guys gathered around me as the spirits faded away completely. I caught one last glimpse of Oscar's face, his mouth twisted as if he wasn't sure he wanted this, but there was something bright and almost hopeful in his eyes. It sparked an answering hope in me in the instant before he disappeared completely.

"What the hell?" someone said. As I raised my head, a waft of warmer air carried over me.

It'd been late spring when I'd first entered Roseborne... With all my cycles through this place, it was probably late summer in the real world by now. The real world that was taking back this campus.

The lawn's grass sprouted up even taller and wilder beneath the moonlight. The bodies that had fallen there, lifeless, faded away into the earth. Those few, I hadn't saved in time.

Before our eyes, the Victorian mansion where we'd endured so much torment crumbled. Half of its roof collapsed; the windows went dark, some of them glinting with broken glass. The corner of the sitting room caved in. The front door toppled off its frame. Within a matter of seconds, the building transformed from the heart of the school into a ruin.

The ruin it'd been all along underneath the supernatural power that had sustained Roseborne?

The gate behind me wavered in a waft of hot breeze, its hinges squeaking. I hauled myself to my feet with Elias grasping one of my arms, Jenson the other. The weakness that had gripped Elias earlier appeared to have left him. Nothing but joy showed in his posture now.

The other students milled around us in a daze of relieved confusion. Violet emerged from the crowd, her scars still deep as ever but no longer angrily raw. Someone had made sure she escaped after all.

She shot me a crooked smile. "You managed it. You broke them."

"No," I said, with a pang as I thought of Winston. "I gave them the chance to put themselves back together."

"Well… Thank you." She peered past me toward the road beyond. "I guess now we all get to find out what's waiting for us out there. It can't be any worse than what we dealt with in here."

Other students came up beside her to stare at me. A couple of them touched my arms briefly as if confirming that *I* was really here would help convince them of the rest. "Thank you," one and another murmured, some sounding teary, others a little terrified. "Thank you."

I wasn't sure I deserved all that gratitude. Had I managed this coup because I was stronger or smarter, or just because I'd had something in me they hadn't through no fault of their own? It wasn't as if I could claim to be *better*.

But I wanted to be. I wanted all of us to be.

"You know what?" I said, pitching my voice just loud enough to carry across the lawn. "The best way you can thank me is to go out there and fix the crap you did that made Roseborne notice you. Help as many people as you ever hurt. Build things instead of breaking them. Whatever you have to do. Just… Don't let what happened here ever happen again."

I stepped to the side as they started to stream out past the walls. Between the uneasy whispers between them and the nervous glances, I didn't know how much that plea had sunk in or how many of them would follow it. Roseborne had shaken us all, but how much would those effects linger once our time at the college seemed like nothing more than an extended nightmare?

I guessed we'd each find out for ourselves.

A glimmer of green caught my gaze through the doorway of the crumpled mansion. As the others left, I moved toward it with an itch of curiosity and a pinch of grief. The three guys came with me in silence.

I stopped on the threshold. Where Cade had fallen— where he'd *died*—his body had vanished. In his place, sprouting up from the spot where the knife had dug into his chest, a sapling had stretched its branches and opened its first leaves.

Not a rosebush this time. I spotted a few green shapes amid the leaves. It was a lime tree, already bearing fruit.

Keeping a careful eye on the cracked ceiling, I edged across the floor and plucked off one of the limes. A faint warmth emanated from it into my hand. My chest constricted.

"Thank you," I said quietly. Despite all the things I could be angry at Cade for, I was grateful for just as many. Then I turned toward Ryo, Jenson, and Elias where they were waiting in the doorway.

"Let's go home."

# CHAPTER TWENTY-SIX

*One year later*

*Trix*

The late-afternoon sun streamed down into the backyard, the summer warmth drawing a rich scent from the garden's soil. I sat back on my heels where I'd been weeding the plot closest to the patio and tipped my face to the light. Even all these months after my short time under Roseborne's perpetually clouded sky, I took immense pleasure in soaking up the natural glow whenever I could.

We'd moved into this house a couple of months ago at the beginning of the summer, but I was pretty happy with how much I'd managed to do with the yard already. Even though I spent most of my weekdays landscaping and consulting on other people's gardens, getting to putter around in my own was a welcome change. No outside expectations to meet, no justifications needing to be made. The guys were pleased with whatever I came up with.

I tugged out the last few weeds and then shed my gloves. Speaking of the guys, they should be home soon—hopefully with good news. Ryo had already bought the ingredients to make a dinner that would either be in celebration or consolation.

On my way to the back deck, I stopped to check on the two potted lime trees positioned on either side of the steps. A citrus plant grown from seeds wouldn't normally bear fruit after just a year, but limes hung in abundance from their branches. The tree I'd taken the original fruit from had been a little more than natural, after all.

I plucked one of the limes for Ryo's use and let my fingers run over the tree's delicate leaves. These weren't the only two plants I'd been able to grow from the seeds in the fruit I'd brought with me from Roseborne, but I'd found homes for the others with various clients—the ones I thought would most appreciate a tiny bit of magic in their lives. These two trees remained, though, like Cade and I had stuck together through so much of our childhood. I liked to think of them as the best parts of him getting to flourish in a way he'd have enjoyed if he knew.

Someone needed to remember him, to honor his good side one way or another. I'd discovered as soon as we'd gotten back to the real world that because Cade had died in Roseborne's grasp, the college had taken all memories of him with it, just like it must have the rest of its ultimate victims. The Monroes still thought I was the only kid they'd fostered in the past few years. No one had any idea Cade had ever existed except for me and the other survivors.

I'd just come into the kitchen when the front door clicked open. I set down the lime by the cutting board and hurried over to meet my guys.

Elias came in first, with a grin that told me we were going to be celebrating, not consoling ourselves, tonight. He was wearing one of those fitted suits he'd favored for as long as I'd known him, but over the past several months as he'd branched out with new ideas about what kind of business he wanted to create and how to run it, he'd looked increasingly relaxed even in those formal clothes.

"They went for it?" I said, lighting up in turn.

"We're all set. In just a few months, those kids are going to get the opportunity of a lifetime." He grabbed my hand and tugged me to him for a kiss.

When we'd first started picking up the pieces of our lives, Elias had decided that what mattered most to him was reaching out to young people in situations like his own and his sister's. He'd started by seeking out kids and teens who might not have been getting the most or the best guidance at home, but who had strong opinions and ideas they could make something of themselves with if they had help finding their direction. Through sponsorships and grants, he'd gradually built a youth leadership organization that offered paid classes and enrichment to the kids whose families could afford it while funding poorer kids who'd shown aptitude. Today he and a few members of the board, including the friend he'd cut out of his past business venture, had gone to speak with a major entertainment corporation about a partnership.

Two other board members came up on either side of me to claim their own congratulatory kisses. Jenson beamed at me unreservedly, all his layers of protective facade long shed as he'd come into his own too. He now put his con artist skills to more legitimate use, teaching workshops for Elias's company on how to project confidence and network effectively as well as acting as an occasional security consultant for businesses wanting to test their employees.

I bobbed on my toes to kiss him with full enthusiasm and then turned to Ryo. His smile was as bright and gentle as ever, but without the hint of melancholy that had clung to him so often at Roseborne. He hadn't totally settled into a definite line of work, preferring to take his opportunities as they came these days, but when he wasn't refurbishing décor I could use for my clients or leading Elias's pupils in craft-related classes, he volunteered with a charity that sent former addicts into schools to share their experiences and hopefully help guide vulnerable students on a better path. Each time he came back from one of those sessions, I saw a little more weight lifted from his shoulders.

He captured my mouth with a tender press and then headed toward the kitchen with his usual upbeat energy. "Time to get cooking!"

It'd taken some time for the four of us to find a balance back in the real world. We'd all come from different towns or cities; none of us had a living space of our own except Elias, and his condo had passed to new owners while he'd been in Roseborne's limbo, with no recourse to get it back even now that the evidence of his existence had reformed in people's minds and computer databases. Roseborne's magic appeared to adjust for the long absences in a way that made everyone around us believe we'd been gone for normal if misguided reasons.

So we'd stuck together, through the early squabbles and moments of uncertainty, as we'd figured out our ways back onto our feet with some help from Elias's substantial savings, which hadn't disappeared or been taken over. From a motel room to an apartment and now this house, as we'd become more sure of ourselves and what we meant to each other, we'd discovered an equilibrium that felt easier than I'd ever have imagined my life could.

Ryo got to work prepping the steaks while giving light-hearted orders to the rest of us to chop this vegetable or combine this ingredient and that one, and we all followed his lead without argument. Each of us had our strengths, and he was definitely the king of the kitchen.

Jenson stole a piece of caramelized onion from the pan just before Ryo dropped in the first two steaks. He licked his fingers appreciatively. "Where'd you learn this one?"

A shadow did cross Ryo's face then, if only for a second. "It's my dad's recipe," he said, quick and quiet, and offered a shrug as if to say it wasn't any big deal.

He'd reached out to his parents tentatively since we'd escaped Roseborne. From what he'd said, they'd been confused by his absence, relieved he was okay, but hesitant to see him. Too much pain lingered, raw from the years of hurt and the additional years when they'd been left adrift not knowing his fate. But they still talked to him in between the stretches of space he gave them. I thought there was reason to hope they'd eventually forgive him. It might just be a long journey.

Jenson hadn't spoken to his parents at all since he'd returned, declaring them "bad influences I'd rather not invite back in." Elias had gone to speak to his grandfather once and returned looking resigned but satisfied, so I guessed he'd gotten what he needed to out of the confrontation even if the older man hadn't been open to hearing his new perspective.

When dinner was ready, Elias poured wine into the glasses around the table, and we all clinked glasses with a cheers to their successful venture. As we dug into the meal, Jenson narrated the meeting with dramatic flourishes.

"When do you think you can come around and do another gardening session with the kids, Trix?" Ryo asked when the other guy had finished. "I think the younger ones especially get a lot out of that—just seeing they can grow something."

At Elias's enthusiastic nod, I had to smile. "I'm pretty booked up next week, which is awesome—the word of mouth really seems to be spreading—but I think the Friday after that I might be able to keep open. I'm always happy to pass on the green thumb."

The wine gave me a slight, bubbly buzz, and the dinner left me comfortably full but craving a different sort of satisfaction. As soon as we'd finished loading the dishwasher, I wrapped my hand around Elias's tie with a meaningful look I shifted from him to the other two guys. "Time to take the celebration upstairs?"

Jenson tucked his arm around my waist and pressed his lips to my cheek. "That sounds like a perfect idea."

We'd picked this house partly for the expansive back yard and partly for its four bedrooms. The three other than the master were on the smallish side, but considering at least one of the guys usually spent the night in the master with me, all that really mattered was we each had at least some space that was just ours when we needed it.

While I had plenty of one-on-one interludes with my lovers, there was nothing quite as thrilling as enjoying them all at once. We'd found a sort of harmony there too, and the pleasure we could make from *that* collaboration felt like something more than the sum of our parts. Something bigger and sweeter, and not just about physical satisfaction. I treasured the love between me and each of the guys—and the affectionate respect they'd developed for each other—so much that any skeptical glance or judgmental murmur when we were out in public merely rolled off my back.

In the bedroom, the guys surrounded me, choosing their places through some unspoken agreement. Jenson eased his hands up under my shirt as Elias hooked his fingers into the soft fabric to strip it right off me before claiming my mouth. Ryo kissed my shoulder and stroked his fingers over my outer thighs. My hands flitted between each of them, drawing all the passion and pleasure I could from our closeness. And tugging them out of *their* clothes as quickly as I could manage it.

We ended up on the king-sized bed, plenty big for all sorts of fun. Ryo dipped his head between my legs, and I groaned as he slicked his tongue over my sex. Jenson caught the sound with a kiss. I tangled my fingers in his hair, trailed my other hand down Elias's chest to grasp his cock, and arched into Ryo's dedicated mouth.

It only took a minute before I was quaking on the verge of release. Ryo grazed his teeth across my clit, and I came with a surge of pleasure. He kissed his way up my torso as I floated in the aftermath, but we were hardly done yet.

I grasped Elias's hip and urged him over me. As he settled between my thighs, teasing the head of his cock over my opening, I tipped my head toward Ryo to return the favor he'd given me. When I gripped Jenson's erection, he pushed into my hand with an eager stutter of breath.

We found our rhythm easily now, the pulse of Elias thrusting in and out of me echoing through me to my mouth around Ryo's cock, my fingers around Jenson's. Bliss flowed through me with the burn inside, the caresses of so many hands over my body, and the increasingly urgent sounds of my lovers' pleasure. I didn't want it to end, and yet the ending was the best part.

It came over us in a wave. My climax brought my lips tighter around Ryo's length, my fingers gripping Jenson's erection even more firmly, and they came within seconds of each other with a chorus of stuttered breath. Elias groaned and stiffened as he followed us into that shared ecstasy.

They sprawled around me on the bed, cocooning me in heat and mutual adoration. I snuggled my head close to Jenson's, slipped my arm around Ryo's, nestled my legs against Elias's.

A year ago, we'd been four broken people struggling to believe we even had enough pieces left of ourselves to be someone whole. Now, my heart was filled to bursting.

"This," I said. "This is home."

"I take it you like the house," Elias said wryly.

I nudged him with my toes. "No. Being with the three of you. No matter where we are—that's home."

Jenson lifted his head to press a kiss to my temple. "No arguments here. There's nowhere else I'd rather be." I could still hear a thread of elation in his words every time he had the chance to declare his affection openly, without needing to twist the words around a liar's curse.

Ryo twined his fingers with mine and cuddled closer. "And we only had to go through hell to find it."

I had to laugh, but what he'd said was true. Roseborne *had* put us through hell. But we'd made something wonderful over the ashes of that awful place, and that was all the proof I needed that whatever else was coming our way, we'd make it through all right.

# ABOUT THE AUTHOR

Eva Chase lives in Canada with her family. She loves stories both swoony and supernatural, and strong women and the men who appreciate them. Along with the Cursed Studies trilogy, she is the author of the Royals of Villain Academy series, the Moriarty's Men series, the Looking Glass Curse trilogy, the Their Dark Valkyrie series, the Witch's Consorts series, the Dragon Shifter's Mates series, the Demons of Fame Romance series, the Legends Reborn trilogy, and the Alpha Project Psychic Romance series.

*Connect with Eva online:*
www.evachase.com
eva@evachase.com